For Nigel and Emma

Also available by Karen Banfield

A Touch of Drama at Bedtime – a short story collection

Murder Around the Clock (Interactive version) – a murder mystery play. Published by Lazy Bee Scripts

Performances of full length Plays:

Murder is Addressed at Dembe Theatre, Tring and Limelight Theatre, Aylesbury in March 2025

A further Murder Mystery is scheduled for March 2026

The Conman with a Conscience – a play about money and morals at the Limelight Theatre, Aylesbury in October 2025

Fourteen Full length Murder Mystery plays available for performance, enquiries to Karen.banfield67@gmail.com

https://www.facebook.com/KarenBanfieldWriter

A Little Crime at Bedtime

a Short Story Collection

Karen Banfield

First published in 2024

by Banfield Publishing

All rights reserved

© Karen Banfield 2024

The moral right of Karen Banfield to be identified as the author of this work has been asserted by her in accordance with Section 77 of the Copyright, Designs and Patents Act 1988

This book is sold subject to the condition that it shall not, by way of trade or otherwise, be lent, re-sold, hired out or otherwise circulated without the author's prior consent in any form of binding or cover other than that in which it is published and without a similar condition including this condition being imposed on the subsequent purchaser.

This book is a work of fiction. Names, characters and incidents are the product of the author's imagination. Any resemblance to actual events or persons living, or dead, is coincidental.

Printed in Great Britain by Amazon

Cover design by Emma Tuohy via Canva and AI

ISBN: 9798300112257

Contents

Never Forget a Face	1
Hidden in Plain Sight	9
My Secret Hobby	17
Doing the Right Thing	19
Kiss it Better	29
Feathers	37
The Best Thing about Dying	41
An Eye for an Eye	47
The Tea Service	53
Accidental Death	59
Me and Mr G	65
Centre Stage	71
Seen through a Window	77
The Confession	79
Unwanted Intruder	97
Forgiving Nature	101
Retire for Life	107
Brotherly Love	125
Being Covered	129
It's all thanks to Campion	133

Never Forget a Face *(Gina's Tale)*

I recognised him straight away. I was good at faces, even if I couldn't remember names. But this time I knew both, as clearly as if the last time we'd met, was yesterday. If I hadn't had such a rough time, perhaps I would have reacted differently. If only I hadn't realised there was someone to blame.

The chemo was gruelling, and I can picture my GP's face as she said she wouldn't lie to me, I was at an advanced stage and so it would be tough. But I should give it a go. I might well cope quite well and it would give me many more years. As I sat through treatment, I asked myself over and over if I really wanted many more years. Had the years I already experienced been so good that I wanted more of them? Not really. I could see I was just existing, yet my survival instinct wouldn't let me give up. It wouldn't allow me the luxury of hiding under the duvet when I had to get going for yet another hospital appointment.

My life was well ordered and from the outside, those that knew me would think I was perfectly happy. But maybe that was because I never let anyone know me at all. They saw the cheery smile when I went into the office, the diligent worker sorting out the company's payroll and the sympathetic colleague listening to the troubles of the others over lunch. If pushed, they might say I preferred my own company. That they'd never seen me with a boyfriend but that I was always busy with my allotment and a regular at the gardening club. Even the other members there, some of whom I must have known for twenty years, they wouldn't be able to tell you much about my life beyond the superficial. And that's just as I wanted it. I didn't want anyone knowing what really went on in my head.

I wouldn't have even known what caused the cancer, if I hadn't made a casual remark when I was leaving Dr Granger's office. I said, 'I hear that boys are getting this vaccine as well as girls now, but I don't really understand why.' It's not as if they can get cervical cancer.

'No, she said but they can carry the virus. And it can make them ill too, in different places.'

'What do you mean virus?' I asked. I hadn't ever heard of cancer being caused by a virus. I thought it was from things you ate or breathed in, like smoking.

I almost laughed. 'So I caught it like a cold. Just walking around, breathing in the same air that someone else has just breathed out, with the virus in their breath.'

'No, that's not how HPV is transmitted. HPV is only passed on through sexual contact.'

I sat down, because at that moment, I thought I would faint. Everything became unreal as memories and images forced their way through my mind, uninvited after being long buried.

'Are you all right?' I heard her ask and I must have nodded as I was out of the room before she could tell me to sit down or explain how I felt. Because I didn't know how I felt. I managed to get myself to the car and close the door before I burst into tears.

I couldn't remember the last time I cried like that. Not since I was a child. Not since, well, I suppose it made sense that the same emotion would flood me now as it did then. After all, the two events had the same cause.

His name was William Bradbury, and he was in my year. He let his friends call him Billy, but would thump anyone else who tried. Even the teachers didn't dare. I was plain and awkward. Not particularly good at anything, not particularly liked or disliked and so school had been bearable even if it was tedious. That was until William started talking to me. At first he always seemed to be behind me in the queue in the cafeteria. He first commented on which culinary failures to steer clear of and then he got more personal when he said he was surprised I ate chips, when I didn't have any spots and that I had nice skin. I felt myself go red and not knowing how to get out of it, I carried on asking for chips from the dinner lady, but that was the last time I did. I didn't want to risk spots suddenly appearing. I didn't want to spoil my nice skin.

I asked Mum if I could borrow some of her moisturiser to put on at night and she was happy to see her frumpy little girl starting to take an interest in herself at last. She'd tried to show me how to put a little bit of mascara on a few months before, but I hadn't wanted to. I didn't have the confidence to think boys would be interested in me. My reasoning was that if I went 'round with makeup on, it sent a message that I thought myself attractive. And that could have led to them laughing at me. I'd seen how other girls had been treated, how they were called names and given a hard time for starting to act like women. Perhaps that's why he targeted me. Because I wasn't pushing myself forward, in fact the opposite, I was hiding in the shadows. Despite the slight attention of William, I wasn't ready to do any more than moisturise my face and my hands. After all no one could see they felt all soft, but should he want to hold my hand, I'd be ready.

Given his daily appearance behind me, I wasn't completely surprised when he asked to sit next to me. I nodded and we found the end of a bench free, to sit opposite. I suddenly lost my appetite and wondered how on earth I could eat anything in front of him.

'You're Gina, aren't you.' He said, matter-of-factly.
'Yes,' I replied.
'You can call me Billy.'

I blushed and wanted to repeat his name back to him, but I found myself unable to get the word out. I tried to eat a small piece of lettuce to hide my embarrassment but even that was hard to swallow. He chatted on, not requiring more than a smile in return whilst he talked about himself and his plans for the future. He wasn't going to stay on at sixth form, he was going to do an apprenticeship at the garage. His dad knew the supervisor there and they were going to pay for him to learn to drive in a few months' time. He couldn't wait to get himself a set of wheels. And how I longed to be sitting beside him in some open-top sports car that turned people's heads when we sped past.

Two days later he asked if I wanted to meet him for a coffee in town on Thursday after school. I managed to say that would be great, whilst wondering how to tell him I didn't like the taste of coffee. I'd try some again at home tonight and see if I could get used to it. After all, surely it was only children that didn't drink it.

I managed to drink two cups of coffee that evening and three the night after, having doused each of them liberally with lots of milk and sugar. I couldn't say I liked it, but I could tolerate it. I posed in front of the mirror with a cup, making sure I didn't pull any kind of funny expression when the bitter liquid hit my tongue. I thought I looked quite sophisticated. Well as much as any sixteen-year-old could wearing a school uniform and hair in a ponytail. Having decided I could pass for an experienced coffee drinker, I turned my attention to my hair and decided I looked oldest when it was down around my shoulders. It was a honey brown that I'd always rather liked, and I hoped he would too, if he ran his fingers through it. I was excited by the possibility.

I debated on whether or not to wear lipstick, trying to work out if Mum had anything vaguely suitable. I'd looked through her collection and there was a pale reddish pink that wasn't too noticeable. I put it in my pocket and decided I wouldn't ask her, as I didn't want to have to tell her about Billy. She'd want to be really embarrassing and tell me to invite him round for tea. I pinched the mascara she'd shown me before as well and practiced putting on just enough to make my lashes stand out a bit, without going over the top.

I arrived at the coffee shop and could see through the window he wasn't inside. I pretended to read the menu and look at the cakes on display until he arrived.

'Hi' I said when he turned up and we went inside together.

'White coffee please,' I asked the waitress but was rather disappointed when Billy ordered a chocolate milkshake.

'It's good to have lots of protein,' he explained, 'helps build up muscle strength.' He looked straight at me and seemed to enjoy me blushing.

'Do you do weightlifting?' I asked, not thinking how I'd react whichever way he answered.

'Don't need to,' he said, 'naturally strong, I am.' He leaned in closer, 'never had any complaints.

I was blushing even more now and desperately trying to think of a better topic of conversation. After forcing the burning hot drink down a few sips, I remembered what he'd said about driving.

'What car would you like, when you can afford one?' I asked, pleased with a question that I thought was quite sophisticated. Unfortunately I didn't know any of the makes that he mentioned, so I just nodded.

Billy asked if I fancied going to the pictures and I said, 'Sure, but I'll need to tell Mum. She'll fuss if I'm not back when she's expecting me.'

'There's a phone box on the corner,' he pointed out and I rang her and told her I was out with Natalie and might have my tea with her. Mum was fine and now wouldn't be asking me intrusive questions when I got back.

I don't remember much about the film. I kept sneaking a look at Billy, trying to work out how I'd been lucky enough to be noticed by him. There were plenty of other girls more attractive than me, that would have gladly gone out with him. He put his arm around me and we shared a bag of popcorn. About halfway through he leant over and kissed me. I smiled at him, delighted at the tingling I felt on my lips. When he started running his hand under my blouse and into my bra I didn't object and started relishing the reckless feeling of doing what felt right instead of listening to the voice that told me it was wrong. We'd been sitting in the back row, right up in the far corner, well away from anyone else. There weren't very many people there anyway.

'You're beautiful, you know that?' He said. I could smell the popcorn on his breath and felt my heart race at hearing the words I'd longed to hear, even though I hadn't realised that until just that moment.

'Shall we?' He asked and for a moment I didn't know what he was asking and then suddenly I knew. And I wanted to, despite knowing I shouldn't, when I hardly knew him. But he'd said I was beautiful, and he wanted me. He wanted to make love to me, not to any of those other, prettier girls. He held my hand and guided me to lying down on the floor, between the rows of seats, and he quickly knelt down next to me. I tried not to notice the chewing gum stuck to the underside of the seat, the chocolate wrappers and sticky carpet. These weren't important, not now that Billy had chosen to be with me.

In a panic I whispered to him 'I don't want to get pregnant.' But he just replied I couldn't if it was my first time, and I nodded because he'd guessed correctly. He knew what to do and I lay there and let him, trying to enjoy it despite the discomfort and feeling the pain I'd heard about. I was just starting to get used to being in the cramped space and his weight on me, when he made a noise I'd never heard before. He stopped and tucking himself in, he got up. I tried not to look disappointed and pretended I'd known that was exactly what it would be like. We sat back on our seats and watched the rest of the film.

Outside the cinema, he waved at me and said, 'bye', hurrying round the corner and down the hill. I started to say something, but he was out of earshot by the time I'd thought of anything. 'Bye,' I said, standing alone on the pavement, dazed.

I couldn't wait for lunchtime the next day and I looked 'round for Billy. I caught sight of him and put my hand up to wave, but he looked through me as if he didn't know me. I thought he couldn't have seen me and when I had my tray of food I walked back towards where he was. But I stopped in my tracks when I heard him talking to the girl in front of him.

'I'm surprised you eat chips, since you've got such nice skin.' He told her and she giggled. That's when I knew he had seen me waving at him but that I had already been replaced. I'd obviously been a big disappointment yesterday and I felt the tears start to sting in my eyes. I virtually dropped my tray on the nearest table and ran out of the cafeteria before he saw my humiliation written all over my face.

I plucked up the courage to ask mum if you could get pregnant on your first time and she'd said of course you could, but not that I'd need to worry about that for ages yet. I'd nodded and spent the next month in dread that I'd be expecting his baby on top of everything else. It must have been about a week before the end of the summer term, when I overheard him bragging to his friends.

'Told you. Sixteen years old, so sixteen girls before I leave this dump.' And he'd rattled off the names. I'd heard of them all and they seemed to follow a pattern. They were like me, quiet, maybe a bit plain and desperately longing for any kind of flattery.

That was the worst summer of my life. Coming to terms with how he'd treated me. I couldn't bear to stay on at school after that, even though I knew he was leaving, I couldn't face bumping into any of his other victims, seeing my own shame reflected in them. So I went to college and then to the firm I'm still with. Whenever a boy showed an interest in me after that, I couldn't help thinking he had ulterior motives, some bet or other that I was there for the taking. Even when the boys became men, I couldn't bring myself to accept the most innocent of invitations. So I lived alone and planned to keep it that way.

The news the doctor had given me was a shock. I knew I should have gone for smear tests when I'd had the letters over the years. But I couldn't bear the thought of being prodded around like that. Whenever I'd thought about it, I could smell the dust on the carpet of the cinema, and popcorn. I'd never been able to eat that since. It's funny how something humiliating can stay with you and make you feel as stupid as you did the day it happened. It had made me avoid anything that would re-live those moments. I hadn't stepped into a cinema since and even going to a theatre was a trial.

So what Billy and I had done squashed between the rows of seats, was responsible for me catching that HPV virus. Because he was the only one I'd had any sexual contact with. He was the one that had given it to me. From one of the other fifteen girls.

I wiped my eyes and thought I was okay to start driving again. I was going to die from this disease, that was no longer in question. Exactly how long I had left was still uncertain, but it wasn't years, probably just months. I was thinking about this and whether I should draw up a bucket list when I saw him as he stepped onto the zebra crossing. For a moment,

I thought I was imagining him, after all I'd just been thinking of him. But he looked real.

I don't quite know what came over me, except I felt a sudden rage. As if everything I'd bottled up from when I was at school had come back in full force. All those years when I had deprived myself of real happiness by not sharing my life with someone special, all those years when I had been suspicious of men and what their agenda really was. Everything seemed to come crashing down on me and without conscious thought, I put my foot full on the accelerator and drove straight at him. He crumpled and lay on the floor in front of me. I sat there, shocked to my very core at what I'd done. I got out of the car and went 'round to him.

'Billy, I'm sorry.' I said as I crouched down beside him.

He mumbled something and I couldn't work out what it was. I leant in closer and that was when I heard what he said. I didn't understand it, but I heard the words. They were in French. Why was Billy speaking in French? I looked again at the face I had hated for nearly forty years and a chill ran through me as I realised I'd run over the wrong man.

Hidden in Plain Sight *(Catherine's Tale)*

My sister Paige was one of those people that everyone liked. She could have any boy she wanted. We both have vibrant ginger hair, but whilst I have mine cut short in a manageable bob, she's let hers grow halfway down her back, like a beautiful auburn cloak. She was always laughing, and often at my expense.

I'd moved out to go to university and so I didn't see Paige as often. When I returned for the holidays I went back to work at the bakery, earning as much as I could so that I could save up for a deposit to rent a flat that would be all mine. Or even better, one to share with Kyle. I'd been with him for over six months, which was much longer than my previous boyfriends. But then he met her and had been charmed by her easy-going nature. Before I knew it, he'd slept with her. When I confronted her, she said it was no big deal, it was only a couple of times, just a bit of fun. She even said I was welcome to have him back, as if he was a jumper she'd borrowed. He said he was sorry of course and asked me to forgive him, but I didn't want him after that. He was tainted.

Since then, I hadn't risked anyone meeting her, but my new boyfriend Nathan was insistent that he wanted to be part of the family.

'I want to meet them all,' he'd said, 'otherwise I'll think you're ashamed of me.'

How wrong he was. It wasn't him I was ashamed of, it was me and what I became around her. When we were alone I could occasionally come up with a witty remark, but being around Paige made my mind go blank. I went back to being the plain one.

My parents could find no fault with her, even when she crashed their car having drunk too much at a party. Or when she had borrowed money from them without ever paying it back. There was always something about her being the youngest, that got her excused from everything.

'You probably did that when you were her age,' they'd say, 'don't be so hard on her.'

Even when I stood up for myself and said I had never behaved like that, they just looked at me surprised. Eventually Mum would say that she and Dad would have forgiven me just the same and that being young's the time for making mistakes. I could follow their logic to a point, but when Paige deliberately set out to take what was mine, it wasn't because she was just immature.

It was to be the Easter holidays when Nathan and I would stay at Mum and Dad's. I'd told him about the earlier times when I'd worked in the bakery and it was as I regaled some of the amusing moments, that I was struck with the idea. I suppose I was a bit premature in planning to kill her, as soon as she met Nathan, without at least waiting to see if he was attracted to her. But I couldn't take the risk. I'd seen it too many times before. Once boys had seen a more beautiful, livelier version of me, they could never look at me the same again. I had such a good chance that Nathan and I could make it, if we were left on our own.

We'd met at the debating society, first competing against each other and then working alongside to form reasoned arguments that the others found hard to attack. He wanted to go into politics once he'd finished his Masters and he knew this was a skill he had to learn as well as he could. And I helped him. We even practised arguing when we went for walks at the weekend, in the country park.

'You have a way of making me think about things, the way no-one else can.' He said, 'it's as if you can step into someone else's shoes, see their point of view and then step back again, to show a better way forward.'

I had never had anyone be pleased with me like that before. It had been the opposite in fact. My parents had said I argued too much and that I should just accept things as they were. No, I reassured myself, I was completely justified in not letting Nathan go the way Kyle had.

Of course I never let on to him how much I hated her. I don't think anyone knew, except maybe Paige herself. Whenever Nathan had asked about her, I'd come across as the proud big sister, who was sadly too busy to see much of her.

But I couldn't get out of the Easter visit and so I had to make this their first and last meeting.

I have always thought that men are easier to manipulate than women and not just over their insatiable weakness for sex. Perhaps it's about their vanity and wanting to be the cleverest. I'd noticed that, if I wanted Nathan to try something new or be more adventurous, I'd have to make him think it was his idea.

So that's what I did next.

'It's a shame I don't work at the bakery anymore as I can't bring Paige back any Easter biscuits. She loved those,' I said. I let the information sink in, knowing he'd want a way to make a good impression. He was an only child and had an idealised view of what it was to have a sibling.

'Why don't I bake her some?' he asked, his face lit up.

'Have you made them before?' I asked, knowing the answer was likely to be no and when it was, I also correctly predicted he'd add that he can easily learn. There was bound to be something on TikTok.

I assured him if he thought he'd have time, she'd love that. He was all pleased with himself and went to look for cookery books. Before long he was opening the kitchen cupboards looking for rarely used ingredients. I'd already thrown away the spices he'd need, in a rubbish bin in the High Street. The magazine from our local supermarket was on the coffee table and because I'd repeatedly folded back the first twelve pages, when Nathan picked it up, it helpfully opened at the page on Easter baking. An advertisement for organic extracts and spices was at the bottom. There was no-one more committed to healthy eating than my boyfriend. I was in the hall when I heard him tear the page out of the magazine, and I allowed myself a smile.

It wasn't really necessary but I couldn't risk bumping into anyone I knew at the supermarket. I didn't want anyone to join the dots up later. Luckily I easily disguised myself with a baseball cap, shoving my noticeable hair inside, and then finishing my anonymity off with jogging clothes. I bought the overpriced bottles of flavouring I needed and was pleased with how well I managed to swap the small navy blue and gold labels over. When I'd done what I needed to with the bottles, I hid them in one of my walking boots.

The evening before we were due to go to my parents, Nathan was excited about his baking. He'd visited the supermarket during his lunch break and bought what he needed. He'd left all the ingredients out on the worktop, and I swapped one bottle over whilst he was getting changed. Despite his love of cooking, he didn't have a good sense of smell or taste, which I'd told him was because he vaped as it wasn't much better than smoking. This time, it would work in my favour as I was relying on him not noticing that there was an intruder in his biscuits. I hoped he'd be overwhelmed with the mixed spice and raisins. I found myself holding my breath when he took his first bite, once they had cooled sufficiently from the oven.

'Delicious,' he pronounced, 'want one?'

'I'd love to but I think we should save them for the family gathering.' I knew the word family would stop him eating any more.

When he was in the bath later that evening, I retrieved one of the miniature bottles from my boot and wiped it clean of my fingerprints. I thought this was probably an unnecessary precaution and without Nathan's prints, that would be suspicious, but nevertheless I couldn't help myself. I poured a few drops into the sink and quietly ran the tap to wash it down. I put the bottle in the cupboard, next to the one of mixed spice then took out the one I'd relabelled as vanilla extract. I hid it inside the same boot I'd used before.

I hardly slept that night. It should have been because I was wracked with guilt at what I was about to do, but to be honest, it was from excitement. From tomorrow, everything would change. The shadow that had been lurking all these years would finally be lifted and I'd no longer have that fear, that she'd be favoured over me.

We pulled up outside the semi that I'd grown up in, at exactly the time we'd said. I knew Paige had already arrived, as her large handbag was open in the hallway, as usual, ready to trip someone up. This normally annoyed me, but today I'd banked on it being there.

The introductions were made and I knew as soon as Nathan saw her, I'd made the right decision. There was just a subtle shift in his interest to her, from the initial setting eyes on her, to him not stopping himself looking at her. I slipped back into the hall whilst she entertained everyone with her tale of the argument she'd had with a parking attendant. Her EpiPen was near the top, as were some cosmetics. I gently nudged the bag onto its side and the pen and a lipstick rolled out. I quietly kicked them both under the grandfather clock and looked down, making sure they were right at the back. I added her black hairbrush for good measure, as it was large enough to hide the pen completely.

I forced myself to eat the roast dinner my parents had cooked and joined in the conversation as normally as I possibly could. It felt an age before it was four o'clock and Nathan suggested his Easter biscuits. Everyone took one, Paige only pausing to ask if it had nuts in.

'No,' Nathan said, 'none in the ingredients and we haven't had any in the house for ages. Catherine told me you're allergic.'

She took a large bite. 'Mmm,' she began and then took another. But her face changed as she looked quizzically at Nathan. 'They taste a bit nutty, are you sure?' she began, before she turned red and put her hand to her throat. She then began trying to gulp air down.

My mother sprang into action. 'Quick! Where's her EpiPen, she's going into shock.' She left the room and I could hear the contents of the handbag being emptied out. I was purposely sitting as far away as possible, so it was natural that Dad and Nathan went ahead of me, crowding round the bag.

I went over to Paige. Rubbing her back and saying soothing words. 'You'll be all right. Just breathe nice and evenly, you'll be fine. Just breathe. We're all here'.

She looked at me, her eyes wide open with fright and the strangest noises coming from her throat. She was holding it now with both hands, as if trying to force her airways open from the outside.

'I can't find it, where is it?' Mum cried. 'Did you bring it with you?' She continued to sift through the heap of contents she'd emptied from Paige's handbag.

'Did you bring it with you?' I asked Paige. I watched her nod before calling out to the hallway, 'she nodded that she did.'

'We should call an ambulance,' Nathan said and started dialling before waiting for an answer.

Paige was making terrible noises, a kind of squeak came out of her as she tried to talk and the loud gasping. I did feel a little sorry for her, but every time I succumbed to that, I just thought of Kyle and stroking her hand became an act.

'Maybe it's in her pocket,' I suggested and started patting her down. I put my hand in all her pockets, hating the used tissues that I emptied out. 'It's not here,' I called back, putting the sound of panic in as much as possible. 'What about a jacket, was she wearing a jacket? Is it hanging up?'

'She wasn't wearing one,' Mum answered.

Paige's eyes were closing now. I was confident she'd be unconscious soon. I put my arm around her and rocked her, as if I was distraught at the terrible distress she was experiencing. I hid my face in her hair, worried I couldn't pull off the right expression for any length of time.

Dad got on his hands and knees and looked under the clock. 'There it is, at the back.' He stretched his arm as far as he could and grasped hold of it.

He pushed me out of the way and stabbed her with the pen, but she didn't react.

I sobbed loudly, 'it's all my fault. I did this to her. She might die because of me.'

'What are you talking about, whatever do you mean?' Mum asked.

'I told Nathan how much she liked Easter biscuits. If I hadn't he wouldn't have baked them.'

The ambulance arrived and they took her away immediately, lights flashing and sirens blaring. Mum and Dad went with her. An hour later Dad rang me and said she hadn't made it. Nathan and I agreed we'd wait until they came home. It was a long couple of hours, but I didn't think I would be convincing at my grieving, if I put the TV on. We sat and held hands, waiting. Once they returned it wasn't much better, so I was glad when it was Nathan that suggested we should make a move and let Mum and Dad have time to themselves.

When we arrived home, the first thing Nathan did, was to look at the bottles in the kitchen cupboard. 'Perhaps one of those fancy organic flavourings had traces of nuts,' he said.

'That's probably it,' I agreed, 'but I bet they didn't bother putting a warning on the label.'

A minute later his face was ashen as he held the small bottle in his hands, that he expected to be vanilla extract. 'It says almond extract,' he said horrified, 'it was all my fault.'

'How on earth did that happen?' I said, sounding all innocent. He picked up the bottle of mixed spice and it was obvious the range of flavourings had very similar navy blue and gold labels. The writing was in italics and hard to read. These were factors I'd taken into account when I'd planned this.

'You can't go blaming yourself,' I said, 'it was an honest mistake.'

He hugged me. 'I can't tell you how sorry I am. I know how much she meant to you.'

I nodded, dabbing a non-existent tear from my eye.

It's been five years now and Mum and Dad seem to be over the shock of it. If they go on too much about how perfect she was, I revert to my routine of it all being my fault. I'd remind them that she loved those biscuits and I'd introduced her to them when I'd worked at the bakery. Anxious to help their remaining daughter, they'd switch to playing that down and reassuring me it was an accident.

Nathan is now bound to me forever. After all, how could he leave me after what'd he'd done? He thinks I'm so forgiving.

Sometimes I look at his face when he's asleep and see frown lines that shouldn't be there at his age. I should feel guilty, but I don't. After all, it's not my fault she had to die. She just couldn't be trusted.

My Secret Hobby *(Liam's Tale)*

I guarantee no one else in the room liked the sound of Milton Keynes for the reasons I did. The firm had grown beyond anyone's expectations and a relocation out of London was needed.

'Close enough to commute,' Bob the director said, 'for anyone wanting to still live around here.' He clicked through the slides. 'But when you see what it has on offer, you might well change your minds.'

'Why there, of all places? I've heard it's just a load of roundabouts,' Naz piped up.

'That's for the main roads. They're in a grid, so you can easily find your way from one estate to the next. And it's got these Redways so you can cycle everywhere off the roads.' Bob scrolled through a couple more slides to show them.

But it was the next set that really caught my attention. There were so many different woods and parks as well as nature reserves. They were everywhere. I felt that sense of anticipation, the excitement of planning what I'd come to think of as my secret hobby.

I absolutely loved what I was looking at. It would be just perfect for what I needed. Perfect for burying the bodies.

It was just so difficult to do that in London. There were so many people around, even at night. I'd had a few close shaves even when I'd thought the bit of woodland was off the beaten track. I'd had to hire a car especially as it was impossible to balance anyone on my folding bike.

With the generous relocation package that was being offered, I thought I could buy a car and still rent somewhere reasonable. Bob had already said how Milton Keynes was green in more ways than one, and that there were lots of places to charge electric cars. I thought I might like one of those, as I like to do my bit.

It was no bad thing for me to move around fairly often, otherwise I was more at risk of being found out. It wasn't just luck that meant I hadn't been caught yet. I'd chosen my victims very carefully. They needed to be from abroad, without family and not yet to have had a chance to make any real friends. London had been great for that as there were so many that fitted my criteria. I liked women best. They were so much easier to subdue.

I really needed to know if Milton Keynes was the perfect green paradise I was picturing it to be. I had to keep my voice steady so that I didn't draw any attention.

'Are there many foreigners there?' I didn't want to seem racist, so I added, 'My new girlfriend's Indian and she says she hates going to places where she doesn't blend in.'

'She's got no worries there,' Bob replied, 'it's very multicultural.' He listed some different ethnic restaurants, but I'd stopped listening. I'd heard all I needed to. I couldn't wait.

Doing the Right Thing *(Shannon's Tale)*

It was the hardest thing I ever had to do, leaving her there. Her crumpled face looking at me, with tears streaking down. She lifted her hand a little, as if to reach me and hold me back, but I turned my back, telling her I loved her as I walked out of the door.

Everyone told me I was doing the right thing, that it was for her own good. But it didn't feel that way. Surely she should be at home with me. I wouldn't mind taking a break from work, they'd understand and even if they didn't I would have gladly resigned for her. After all she meant everything to me, she was my Mum. The sweetest person you could ever wish to meet and someone who had sacrificed so many, many things to give me the best life she could. Now the tables were turned, was I giving her the best life I could? I had to listen to the doctors and believe they knew best. She needed specialist care for now and I apparently couldn't give her that at home. If only she could communicate with me.

I visited her in the nursing home every day and a part of me agreed, that they were doing much more than I could. The stroke had affected her in multiple ways and for now she couldn't stand up on her own, so two people were needed to get her in and out of bed. The home was thirty miles from me, but it had many more facilities there than an ordinary care home would have, so it was worth travelling the distance. The massive, sprawling building had once belonged to some playboy that had gone bankrupt, but it meant it had a Jacuzzi and indoor swimming pools that the home had converted into hydrotherapy pools. They said with the right help, she might be able to walk again and even talk. For now it was just sounds. I knew how lucky it was that a place was available at the very time she was ready to be discharged from hospital, but it didn't feel that way. I just felt helpless.

I talked to her all the time. I brought in things from her house and put them around her room, putting her wedding photo right next to her bed. It was normally on her mantelpiece, and she had a habit of touching it every time she walked past it. It was so subtle, a visitor wouldn't have noticed, but I'd seen her do it. Her silent message to Dad that he wasn't forgotten. I wish he'd lived long enough for me to have known him. But a heart attack had stolen him away when I was only three and Rebecca was four.

I didn't like to think about Rebecca too much and the hurt she'd caused Mum so often over the years. The lies she'd told and the times she'd disappeared for days on end, sometimes weeks without a word. Mum would be beside herself with worry and I had to try and track her down. She'd usually joined some group or other, squatting in empty houses whilst they put their campaigns together to save the whale or whatever else their drug-addled brains thought was a worthy cause. Thankfully Rebecca didn't ever get completely hooked on drugs as she could go months without any. Those times, when she was just herself and reliably came home at night, made Mum the happiest she ever was. But it never lasted. My sister was always chasing something that was just around the next corner and never quite catching it.

She'd been gone years now instead of months. The police hadn't been interested beyond filing a report. They said that grown adults were entitled to go somewhere new if they wanted to and they had no obligation to tell their families. They did go as far as mentioning that the Salvation Army could try and help trace people and we gave them a go, but it wasn't successful for us. I couldn't comprehend how Rebecca could be so selfish, when she owed everything to Mum, a loving home, treats for her birthday and going to good schools where the teachers actually cared. It was a mystery why she became what she had. I thought of all the times I'd envied her when we were young, that fact that she hadn't needed to have even one filling and that I was the one to have my face littered with acne whilst she had the perfect smiling face. Maybe she envied my better exam results, I don't know. She never said. It was after the last time she went, that Mum seemed to change. To retreat into herself and have a permanent air of sadness about her.

I still missed the old version of Rebecca. After all, with only a year between us we'd naturally been inseparable as children. She didn't seem to mind that I needed help to keep up with whatever she was doing, she was actually always patient with me. That was until it came to boyfriends. That's when it all changed.

I remember chatting to one of them, Connor his name was, and he said something to make me laugh, just as she walked into the room. She stared at me for the longest time and then told Connor it was time they were going. It was when she told him not to waste time with me, as I was just a little kid, that I felt really hurt. She met them all at the front door after that, so I never got to meet any of them. Even when I went steady with Johnny, she still wouldn't trust me to be alone with any of hers. I couldn't work out why. I saw them from the bedroom window and they all seemed of a kind. Scruffy and unkempt as if they didn't care about themselves. I wondered if they cared about her at all.

Our relationship had changed forever by the time we had both left school and I didn't think I knew her at all anymore. I have no idea why she changed so much. I asked Mum and she seemed just as much in the dark as I was. And now that Mum has had that stroke, I wish my sister was here to help me. Not the adult version of my sister, the one I'd grown up with.

The staff at the nursing home kept trying to reassure me that Mum was making good progress and that she seemed more settled. The physio team had worked hard with her and she could take a few steps now, but was still working on helping her get herself upright on her own. She could lift both arms up, although her coordination was still off and she couldn't seem to locate what she wanted to with her hands. What frustrated us all, was that she still wasn't able to talk. The speech therapist said that she was still making progress and that the sounds she was forming were becoming clearer and it was still possible she could converse again. We just needed to be patient.

They were concerned about how little she was eating, and they encouraged me to think of foods she was fond of and to bring in any treats that might tempt her. They assured me she could swallow without risk of choking, it was a matter of getting her to want to eat. I scoured the supermarkets after that, trying to find things to take in. I brought in Jaffa cakes and her favourite double chocolate chip cookies and sat both on her bedside. I thought the pictures on the boxes might look appealing to her.

I asked if they'd tried her in the fancy hydrotherapy suite and they told me she was scheduled to go in three days' time. I warned them she couldn't swim, so she might put up some resistance if she didn't know what they were trying to do with her. They surprised me then by saying how much they thought she was now able to understand and that they had good reason to think she was quite aware of what had happened to her. I was so relieved because I hadn't been able to see that she had that recognition. I realised how right the doctors had been, she really had needed specialists to work with her. I bought the staff boxes of chocolates next time I visited, thinking how easy it was for them to not be valued.

When I arrived one morning, the senior care worker Maria, caught me as I made my way towards Mum's room.

'Shannon, I'm glad I've seen you first. I have some good news.' She beamed at me.

'Oh yes' I replied excited at the prospect.

'Your mum has managed to say a word. Really very clearly'

'That's wonderful. What did she say?' I asked.

'Becks' Maria replied. 'We don't know who that might be though. Do you?'

My heart sank. What on earth had made Mum want her now? 'That's my sister. Rebecca. I used to call her that when I was young.'

'Well see if she can come and visit. I know not all relatives can face seeing someone they love when they're first unwell. But she's getting stronger all the time.'

'I don't know where she is though. She went off and didn't get in touch.'

'Oh that's a shame.' Maria replied, clearly unconvinced that I couldn't find her if I tried. 'Maybe try Facebook?'

'Yes, all right, I will.' I said, knowing it would be futile. I'd tried it all before, over and over. I took the view that she didn't want to be found and that's why she hadn't left a trail behind. Mum still lived in the same house, so Rebecca could find us whenever she wanted. I hurried on to Mum's room and smiled at her as I started to hope that soon I'd get all of her back again. But she didn't speak again during my visit, and I had to make do with sounds that had no meaning. I could ask her questions and she could nod and shake her head, but she didn't always respond and I didn't know if she was too tired or too confused. I knew I had to rein myself in as the staff pointed out to me on several occasions that I tried to ask too much in one go. Even the flash cards that we used for her to point out different things and words, weren't helping today.

'Mum,' I said, rather nervously, 'were you asking after Rebecca?' I waited for her to nod or shake her head, but she just looked down. When she looked up again, the sadness was evident in her face and I didn't know what to do for the best. I tried to jolly her out of it by talking about the hydro session she was going to have. I tried to joke that maybe one of the male carers would get in the water with her in some tight fitting swimming trunks if she was lucky. But she looked away, uninterested.

I went through the routine all over again. Ringing the numbers of people who had already told me time and again that they didn't know where Rebecca was. I looked on every social media site I could find and posted on my own Facebook account that Mum was asking to see her and could she get in touch. I trawled the streets, trying all kinds of places that I thought squatters might be in, but I just got indifference or insults from those I met. I filled out the Salvation Army forms again. I didn't know where else to try and I felt under such pressure to find her every time I went to visit, what with Maria always asking how I'd got on. I told her what I'd been doing, except visiting the squats, because I didn't think Mum would want everyone knowing that's what she'd sunk to. Despite this, Maria still didn't seem to believe me.

'We think she said it again yesterday' Maria said. 'But we're not as sure as the first time.'

If Mum wanted to see her, I just couldn't let her down. It could be just the catalyst she needed to jump-start her recovery.

I stopped in town to get some bits of shopping after the visit and walked past a poster of a local band that were appearing at The Queens Head pub. The girl holding a guitar had the essence of Rebecca about her and for a moment my heart leapt and I thought I'd found her. But as I looked closely, it was clear it wasn't her. For one thing she was at least 10 years too young and not tall enough. But it gave me the idea.

I went into three charity shops before I had everything I needed. A large black baggy top and long black skirt. There were some clip-on hair extensions that were still in their packet so obviously someone wasn't brave enough to give them a go, plus a floppy black hat. I'd chosen a bright bead necklace and even found some sunglasses that were just a hint of a grey colour, so could pass for prescription ones that were reacting to the light. I finally visited the chemist for some really dark red lipstick and black eyeliner. I tried it on at home and congratulated myself at how unlike me I looked. And how much I imagined Rebecca looked now.

I had trouble driving to the nursing home as the long skirt kept catching under the back of my shoe when I lifted it to de-clutch and brake. This is exactly why I wear trousers, I reminded myself. When I eventually arrived, I felt so nervous, my mouth was completely dry as if I'd just eaten a whole packet of cream crackers. I made myself go inside and adjusted my walk into the confident swagger I imagined she'd have. At the desk I waited and told the receptionist that I was Rebecca to see Molly Johnson, my Mum. She told me room 44 and I went to turn to go there when I remembered that the place should be unfamiliar to me.

'And where is that exactly?' I asked, quite sharply, again trying to differentiate her from the polite person I normally was. She pointed down the corridor and indicated a right turn at the bottom. I strode in that general direction, pretending to look at room numbers on the way.

I suppose I had expected Mum to smile at me, or as much as her uncooperative face would allow. Since she cried quite a lot still, I expected that too, but from joy at seeing her first-born again, after all this time. I hadn't really thought how much I would say to her, in my mind I had only got as far as meeting her. I had the general idea that I'd show up briefly a few times, phone a couple more and then write that I'd followed some new group that needed me desperately to save turtles or something. By then Mum would have been greatly cheered by the knowledge that she was alive and well, thus recover so much better.

Instead she took one look at me and screamed. I hadn't realised she could still make such a noise and I'm not sure she did either. There were tears and a violent shaking of her head. She tried to say something, that sounded a bit like 'can't be', but I couldn't be sure and then the staff arrived.

I was pulled away as it was obvious that the sight of me was upsetting her. I said I'd best go and the shock of seeing me after all these years had obviously been too much, I'd come back another time. And I left hurriedly, before any of the staff could stop me and ask questions.

I got back into the car and sobbed. My poor Mum had been so upset and I'd only gone to all this trouble to make her feel better. My wretched sister, causing trouble again and she wasn't even here.

It would be another year before I found out quite why Mum reacted that way.

When she could get herself in and out of bed, it was agreed she could come home with me. Physio would come and visit her, and I would take her to the speech therapy sessions. She gradually improved and she almost became her old self. There were so many times that I wanted to ask her why she reacted like she did, when she thought Rebecca was standing before her, but I didn't want her having any kind of setback. Eventually I just had to know.

We were sitting in the garden in the middle of August. It was nine in the evening and we'd both had wine with dinner. I sat forming the words in my head, of how best to bring my sister into the conversation. But I couldn't find a way to bring her in gently, so I went straight to asking.

'Mum, why did you get so upset when Rebecca came to visit?'

She sat there, looking into her wine glass and drained the rest down quickly. Whatever I thought she'd say, it wasn't what came out of her.

'I thought she was a ghost.'

'A ghost?' I asked, bewildered. 'In all that black?' I quickly added that the staff had described her to me.

'What other explanation could there be,' she said quietly, 'after all, she was dead.'

'Dead!' I said, much louder than I meant. 'What do you mean?'

'I thought she must have come to take me with her. To the other side, wherever that might be.'

'I know we hadn't heard from her for a long time, but that doesn't mean she isn't still alive somewhere, involved in some lost cause.'

Mum turned to me and looked at me sadly. 'I'm so sorry Shannon, but she is dead.'

'How do you know, did the police come and visit you?' I asked.

'No,' she said. 'I know because I killed her.'

It took me a while to process what she'd just said. 'What do you mean, you killed her? No Mum, nothing you did led to that, she made her own choices.'

She went on, 'Just listen. I tracked her down, about four years ago now. She'd been gone a couple of months by then and she was back in that big condemned house up on the hill overlooking the city. It was waiting for demolition because it wasn't safe, but there were a dozen or so living there in the meantime, but they were all out except her. I asked her why she wanted to stay in such a place and told her she could come home. If she wanted her independence, well then she could rent somewhere to live like everyone else. But she went on about the cause needing everyone to pool all their money for the campaign. Funding some legal advice for an activist that had been arrested somewhere in Africa. She was adamant she wasn't coming home. We were on the landing of the first floor and she was all agitated, saying I needed to stop judging how she lived her life and leave her alone. I'd held her arm and she yanked it away, and with that she fell backwards. She hit the banister and it gave way under her, she fell all the way down onto the tiled floor. When I got to her at the bottom, I could see straight away she'd died. I felt for a pulse, but there was nothing. I just ran. I don't know why, I think I panicked.' She dabbed at her eyes with a tissue and blew her nose.

'Oh Mum. It was an accident. Why didn't you go back, when you'd got over the shock?' I asked.

'I meant to. But then you came home and I couldn't bring myself to tell you.'

'Why not?'

'Because then it might have been real. She really would be dead, not missing in a squat somewhere or on a protest march at the other end of the country. Until I uttered the words to anyone, I could pretend it hadn't happened.'

'You poor thing having to carry this around with you.' I hugged her whilst she cried and cried.

'I thought the police would come 'round and tell us that her body had been discovered. I thought we could grieve together. I thought I might just have a day or two with her alive in my mind, until I had to face up to reality. Only they never came. So I could never tell you.'

'She probably never had anything to identify herself.' I said, 'She called herself different names sometimes, didn't she. Flower names. They probably couldn't work out who she really was. And although on TV they use dental records for that, she'd have needed to have had some work done, wouldn't she. She never even had an x-ray or filling.'

'Shannon, I'm so sorry. I thought I was doing the right thing keeping quiet.' Mum sobbed.

'Just like I did when I tried to impersonate her at the hospital.'

She sat bolt upright. 'It was you!'

'Yes, I thought she could make some brief appearances and then write to you when she disappeared again.'

We hugged and sobbed for the Rebecca we'd both loved and lost.

I pulled away from her as a thought suddenly occurred to me. 'Mum, if you knew she was dead, why did you call out her name?'

'I didn't,' she said.

'They told me you said Becks. And the first time you were really clear.'

'I didn't say Becks, for Rebecca. I was hungry. I wanted those cookies you put by my bedside, just a bit too far out of my reach. I was trying to say biscuit.'

Kiss it Better *(Alice's Tale)*

It was seeing the piece of paper that made me anxious. I'd made a coffee, just the way Sam liked it and took it into his home office. I carried a bourbon biscuit in my hand and lingered just long enough to realise he was talking to his boss. He didn't seem to notice my reaction when I saw what he'd written. Written doesn't really describe what I saw, since it was the same letter over and over again. The whole page was covered in x's, fainter at the top and darker at the bottom of the paper where it was tearing from the force of the pen.

'Why do you write x's when you're on the phone?' I once asked him, only a few weeks after I'd moved in.

'It's not an x. It's a cross, for when I'm cross,' he said smiling.

'I can't imagine you being that.' I'd laughed and called him a pussycat.

He'd meowed and we'd cuddled in a state of bliss that didn't really last very long at all. I never did work out what changed him, I could only conclude he'd been like it all along and just masked his true identity in our early days.

Whenever he hurt me, he'd always say he was sorry afterwards. I asked him why he got so angry, and he blamed work. That they were treating him unfairly, not respecting him. And then apparently I'd done the same at home. I'd sobbed, asking him what he meant, what had I done and the most sense I could get was that I was always going on at him. I tried so hard not to, but it was never enough.

When Henry arrived, things got better again. I dared to hope that by Sam being a parent, he'd be fulfilled and feel important. I'd started to recognise that his outbursts were worse when a younger employee was more senior than him, so they got to order Sam around.

I knew enough about bullies to understand it was power and control they craved and so I tried to give that to him whenever I could.

'Do you think this car seat would be ok?' I asked, showing him a cheap one I had no intention of buying.

'No, no, no look at those reviews. Let me look.' He'd said and chosen one that, unbeknown to him, was on my shortlist.

'Henry doesn't know how lucky he is to have you as his dad.' I'd said and kissed him.

But these tactics didn't last more than a couple of years. Perhaps he saw through them, I don't know. All I knew was that the old Sam was back and so was the constant knot in my stomach. I think I believed my own words that Henry was lucky that he had Sam for a dad or that Henry needed him. He certainly loved him. He'd toddle towards Sam as soon as he came through the door. When he learnt to say daddy, he'd repeat it over and over again. Sam would sweep him up, holding him up high, whizzing him around as if he was a plane. Henry would giggle and beg for more when he was put back down.

Sam usually just walked away from him when he'd had enough, shutting himself in his study to play on his computer. Once Henry managed to push the door open and was completely unprepared for his fun daddy to shout at him to get out. I had to take Henry out into the garden to keep the noise of him crying away from Sam, grabbing the biscuit tin on the way to distract him. I managed to convince him that daddy was startled by the door opening and he hadn't meant to shout. I'd already started to wonder how long I could keep this up. Would Sam be pushed too far one day and do more than just shout at Henry?

And then I would picture them together, Henry in the bath surrounded by bubbles, giggling away. Sam was very inventive at bubble sculptures and stories. The sight of Henry laughing was something I loved most in the world.

Sam had another manager, and this one was even trickier than the last one. He wasn't easily brushed off with excuses and demanded regular progress meetings on Teams. They sometimes went well, if Sam had completed the work he'd been asked to do, but more often than not, he drifted into doing things his way, a better way, which inevitably took longer so he didn't get the results he was asked for.

'Why don't you just do it their way and then when it's not great, you can point out you did suggest an alternative?' I'd not seen him really angry until then. He switched from stressed but calm to something wild. It was the speed at which he grabbed me that took me by surprise.

Even though it's healed now, my little finger aches when I do certain tasks. He always said sorry, but to varying degrees. The more it goes on, the less he's worried by what's happening. In the early days he'd sob and beg me to forgive him. Let me kiss it better, he'd say. Then we would kiss so passionately and sincerely, that I listened to his words, and I did forgive him. He'd trace an x with his finger. The kissing diminished, but the tracing of the x always remained. He wouldn't look me in the eye though.

Seeing the piece of paper today, as terrifying as it was with the amount of x's he'd put down, gave me the strength I needed. I'd known for a long time this day would come, so I knew I just had to make my move.

I didn't have any income of my own, once Henry arrived, Sam didn't want me working. I wasn't worried about going back to the office I'd shared with two other women, sorting out the paperwork in a family-run garage. I'm sure if the office had been anywhere near where the mechanics worked, I'd have been made to give up soon after we met, but as it was, the only one who ever came was in his late sixties and Sam clearly didn't consider him competition. When we moved to this house, it was a long drive to work, so I didn't mind giving that up.

When the law changed, Sam had to pay more tax if I still received Child Benefit, so he told me to stop the claim and he gave me cash for food shopping instead. At first he checked the receipts and the amount of change I gave him back, but he soon got bored with that. So I could sometimes pocket a few coins and give him most of the change he was due. I even bought some budget supermarket brands of cereal and chocolate biscuits, putting them in the branded packets. I watched anxiously to see if he would notice the difference, but he was completely oblivious. I had a few pounds now, but that was all.

I'd wished a million times that I had family nearby, but it was only ever me and Mum anyway, my dad having left after I was born. Mum had gone on holiday with her best friend, to a Greek island and that's where she fell in love with a waiter. Ten years later, they're married running their own bar, aren't very well off but ridiculously happy. I hadn't managed to bring myself to tell Mum how bad life had become. I don't know if it was because I was ashamed, or I didn't want her to worry and then there was that little voice that perhaps I deserved all this, perhaps I was unlovable, in the same way Dad hadn't thought I was. These competing thoughts had whirled in my mind over and over, with me knowing I had to leave, but still desperate to stay. I so wanted Henry to be loved by his mum and dad. For a long time I didn't realise that just because I wanted these things, it didn't mean it was in my control to make them happen. And it was obvious to me now, that the price Henry would have to pay for knowing his dad, would simply be too high.

Henry was asleep and I'd have to wake him soon anyway. With Sam due to start another Teams call in a couple of minutes, I could wake Henry up and just go. I knew if I went, I could never return. I loved this house and all the furniture and ornaments we'd sourced together. We even bought the pictures at an auction, not a fine art one, just ordinary things people no longer wanted and could make a bit of money from. Sam and I had such fun there. We'd look around at everything, making notes in the auction programme as to what we liked and took it in turns to bid.

I longed for those times again, for Sam to be like that again. I'd tried to encourage him to get some help. The times when I would have bruises showing on my face, he was particularly apologetic and I told him I'd only forgive him if he spoke to the GP.

'Why would I want to talk to them?' He'd look up sharply, his expression hardening.

'Well if you are sorry, you won't want to hurt me again.' I said, knowing I was being sharp with him, but I was in pain and angry. I'd thought he was contrite and really did want this to be the last time.

'There's nothing wrong with me,' he snarled, 'it's you winding me up that's the trouble.' He pressed his face close to mine and I could smell the coffee on his breath. 'You're the one who needs looking at, to stop your nagging.'

There was less saying sorry after that, just a kiss where he'd hurt me and then the x traced with his finger. I think deep down he really was sorry, and he wanted to be different, but he didn't have the courage. So I had to find the courage instead, to make him stop once and for all, by leaving. No amount of beautiful décor could possibly make this house feel like a safe home anymore.

I was getting worried this wasn't the right moment. I hadn't made enough of a plan, just the few pounds I'd squirreled away from the grocery money. I didn't have any local friends, the two ladies I was friendly with at my old job, couldn't help me now as one had died and the other moved away. I didn't know where to. Sam hadn't liked me making friends from the ante-natal classes, even though I could really have done with knowing some other new parents, but he made me think we would be happy just the three of us together.

Sam tracked my internet use and all my phone calls, so I had no real opportunity to rekindle any older friendships. The house was set back from others, at the end of a lane, so I didn't even have neighbours to turn to. We didn't know them, we just saw them occasionally as they drove off in their large cars. I can see now how well Sam chose the house and what at first had seemed a secluded paradise for our little family, was really a secluded prison.

I decided I should write Sam a note, to try and head off any suspicions. I said I was taking Henry to the chemist and as I pushed the note across his desk, I saw the second page covered in x's. This helped fuel my resolve. Helpfully the still sleepy Henry scratched at the eczema on his arm. Sam had long since got bored of putting the creams on him and hearing how sore and itchy it was. He nodded his consent, and I whispered to Henry to say goodbye to Daddy, but he wouldn't comply and I couldn't make my feet move. The enormity of what I was trying to do, to take Henry away from his father forever, prevented me from leaving this as their last moment.

'Just a little wave to Daddy.' I whispered and when his attention was focused on the picture on the front of his T-shirt, I held up his hand and waved it for him, as if he was still a baby. I willed Sam not to do anything to stop us or interrogate me as to what exactly I was going to do at the chemist. I felt a sigh of relief when we were able to retreat from the study, unchallenged.

I grabbed my bag and Henry's favourite toy, urging him to get into the pushchair as quickly as he could. I bribed him with chocolate and didn't care he'd look a bit of a mess afterwards. I had to do it now. The sight of the pages of crosses still terrified me, Sam would take his anger out on me later if I was still here. I knew this as well as I knew night followed day. This spurred me on to close the door gently and then walk away at a good pace, but not so fast as to draw attention.

The chemist was about a mile away, in a little row of shops. I went in and took Henry out of the pushchair as he was straining against the straps, which usually meant he was about to object loudly to his confinement. An elderly lady was putting her purse into her handbag before smiling at Henry. He reached his arms out to her and she shook hands with him, making him giggle. I relaxed just a little. I was so close to getting some help.

When the lady had gone, I approached the counter, but didn't recognise the man behind it. I decided to ask for a female assistant and was pleased when he said he'd get Freya. She took me into the consulting room and introduced herself as the pharmacist.

'What's the problem I can help with today then?' she smiled at both of us.

'My husband.'

'What's the matter?' She asked.

'He won't stop hitting me.' And I burst into tears.

'Does he know you are here?'

'Yes. He'll come down if we're gone too long. I just thought you might let me use the phone for a taxi.' I accepted the tissues she thrust towards me and let out what I'd kept in for far too long.

'To leave him?'

I nodded. 'I have to. He'll either start on Henry, or one day he might go too far, and kill me.'

Stay there, I won't be a moment.' Freya said, standing up. 'Turn your phone off for me, would you? Thanks.'

I did as she asked and kept Henry occupied with a lift-the-flap book that he loved, which I always kept in my handbag. He particularly enjoyed it when I whispered the words in his ear and made animal noises as each picture was revealed. He always laughed when I did the wrong noise for the picture and had to correct me. I wondered how far the taxi would take me. I knew I might be eligible to go into a women's refuge and I supposed I'd have to go into the centre of Cambridge to find one. Maybe if I went to the council offices, they could send me to the right place.

After a while Freya returned and she asked me if I had anyone I could stay with. Even if I had the money for a flight to see Mum, I'd never got Henry a passport. Maybe in a while Mum could come over, but I had to get through the next few days before I could see if she could do that. Freya explained she could help me ring the charity to find me a refuge and I was so grateful, that I started crying all over again. That was until I heard a familiar voice in the front of the shop.

'I wonder if you've seen a woman and little boy in a pushchair?' Sam asked, sounding so reasonable. 'I'm a bit worried you see, she's gone out without her medication.'

I looked down at Henry, hoping he hadn't heard, desperate for him not to recognise Daddy's voice. I could whisper in his ear again, but I didn't want to miss what Sam was saying. What if the staff believed him? I couldn't bear to think of what he'd do if I had to go home with him now. Not if he suspected I'd tried to leave him rather than come here for a consultation. I recognised the voice as the assistant I'd first spoken to.

'Sorry, I haven't seen them,' he said.

'Her phone is showing up as here.' Sam said, slightly dropping the false concern in his voice.

'We had a phone handed in. A lady dropped it outside and another customer brought it in. The lady had got into a car apparently, didn't hear our customer trying to call after her.'

'Let me have it.' Sam said.

'I'm very happy to keep it safe for when your wife realises where she dropped it. Or you can tell her when she comes home.' The assistant said.

'I'll take it home, then she's got it as soon as she's back. I'm sure she'll need it.'

'That's not possible I'm afraid. As you say, it's not your property. Now, is there anything else you wanted while you are here?'

I heard the door slam.

Freya looked at me and said, 'I asked Jagdish to say that. It was what you wanted wasn't it?'

'Yes, thank you. Thank you so much.'

'Now you just need a new sim card and turn off your location setting.'

'You sound like you know what you're talking about.' I said, thinking she'd say she's helped other women or even a friend. I wasn't expecting her to pull up her sleeve and show me cigarette burns on the inside of her arm.

Life was difficult for the next few months. We had to move around and had so few possessions, just donated clothes and toys. Eventually we settled in Lincolnshire, and I knew at last I could finally relax. Sam wasn't likely to stumble across us one day, Skegness was the last place he'd visit by choice.

But Henry loved being by the sea and I loved being safe.

Feathers *(Greg's Tale)*

I couldn't wait until it was three o'clock, when I'd finally get to see Charlie. It had been a month since the last time, an excruciatingly long month. Most of that time I'd spent not knowing if I'd be allowed to see him at all. Jade had told me I couldn't and it was only because I threatened to tell Charlie why his left arm wasn't quite straight, that she relented.

I'd agreed it wasn't ideal. This isn't where I wanted him to have to come to. The neighbours are pretty antisocial, and the place has an odd smell to it. Sometimes I think it's the scent of desperation. But since this is where I'm living for the time being, I had to make the best of things. It would be character building for Charlie, well, that's what I tried to convince myself. If nothing else, it would show him he needn't end up like me, if he worked hard at school and made something of himself. He'd live somewhere a whole lot nicer.

At five to three, I was virtually hopping from one foot to the other, I could hardly keep still. Three o'clock finally arrived and we went in and sat down, waiting. I saw him run towards me at the same moment he called 'Daddy'. He flung his little arms around me and hugged tightly. After a minute, he sat next to Jade, who acknowledged me with a nod. Our relationship was on the rocks before this happened and it hadn't survived. I was sad about that but knew that keeping contact with Charlie was the most important thing now. I asked him about school, and he told me all about one of the dinner ladies who gives out mean portions, except to a few that were her favourites. Just like here, I thought, but wisely kept that to myself.

'Daddy, tell me again why Uncle Aaron is called Feathers.'

I had prepared myself for this, knowing he never tired of me telling him the story. I saw Jade roll her eyes, so I knew I had to play this carefully.

'Well,' I began, 'Daddy and Uncle Aaron were very naughty and wanted to take some money that didn't belong to them.'

'Very, very naughty and very stupid' Jade added.

'That's right. Very very naughty and very stupid. Uncle Aaron knew someone called Callum. And Callum told him that there was lots of money in this house.' I didn't explain it was gold jewellery we'd been after, from Callum's grandmother no less. He'd described her as a miserable old witch, who had made his childhood hell with all her rules and making him feel bad whenever he didn't get good grades. And with his mum and dad away a lot with his dad's work, she was the one he spent a lot of time with. So, his revenge was for Aaron and me to break in one Friday night, when she would be out playing bridge.

They lived in this hamlet in the middle of nowhere, where everyone knew each other, and they all met up for this weekly game. The house was supposed to be empty, but if Callum's grandad had stayed behind as he sometimes did, he'd be glued to the television, watching his DVDs of On the Buses. Callum had also told us about their little dog, that would bark if it heard a noise.

'Uncle Aaron and Daddy knew that a man might be in the house with his dog, and we were just supposed to tiptoe past him, to pick up the money.'

'Tell me the bit about the dog, go on tell me.' Charlie was bouncing on his chair, knowing what was coming.

I wished now I'd taken the trouble to read him bedtime stories. I'd have liked seeing him so happy.

'Well, just in case the dog heard us and started barking, Uncle Aaron said it wouldn't be a problem because he could do a brilliant impression of a fox. And when the man heard the fox noise, he'd think the dog was just barking at that.'

'Can he do a good impression of a fox?'

'Oh yes, Uncle Aaron was very good. He could make a noise just like one.'

'Why didn't the man think there was a fox about?'

'Because Uncle Aaron got confused.' At this point, Charlie says the last words with me.

'And instead of a fox, he does the noise of a peacock.' Charlie can't stop laughing and the guards are looking across at me as if I might be breaking some kind of rule. I don't want to spoil the moment, so I wait to see if Charlie calms down.

'So, the man saw us and told us to stay right there because he was going to call the police.' I didn't elaborate that the real reason we did as we were told, was because of a little detail that Callum failed to mention. Grandad, being a farmer, had a shotgun and didn't care about abiding by rules. He never locked it away, always having it close to hand so that he could shoot any rabbits that dared to trespass in his garden. So he was able to whip it out and pointed it straight at us before we'd had a chance to turn 'round.

'Why didn't you run Daddy?'

'Well, we'd been caught and so we needed to be punished for being very naughty.'

'What were you going to do with the money Daddy?' Charlie asked.

He hadn't posed this question before, and I stopped for a minute before answering. The truth was I'd been trying to get a deposit and rent in advance together, so that Jade, Charlie and I could move to a bigger flat. We were squashed in the one bedroom, and it had been driving us all mad. The council didn't care when I asked them for help to get somewhere bigger, they said it would take months if not years and there were people worse off than us. So I wanted to be the big provider for my family and then maybe Jade and I could make a go of it.

I looked across at Jade for support. She knew why, but she wasn't saying anything to help me now. I ploughed on.

'I hadn't really thought about that Charlie.' I said at last.' I was just being greedy. So you need to learn from Daddy's mistake. Not to be greedy and not to take things that don't belong to you.'

'I won't.'

I looked at Jade. 'Will you bring him again? Please.' She looked across and saw how happy he was at seeing me. He didn't seem at all bothered by where he was, so I really hoped she'd say yes.

'Actually Charlie,' I said, 'I need to tell you something. It's about your arm.'

'Don't you dare!' Jade looked at me, fury in her eyes. 'We need to go Charlie.'

'No, Jade, trust me, it'll be all right. Charlie needs to know.' I looked straight at my son. 'You know your left arm doesn't quite go as straight as your right one?'

Charlie obliged by holding his arms out and it was hardly noticeable, but there was something different.

'I need to tell you why that is.' I took a deep breath, 'When you were a tiny baby, I was holding you, having a lovely cuddle after you'd had your bottle, and you fell asleep in my arms. Well, you were so peaceful, and it was so late, I fell asleep too.'

'That's all right. Grown-ups need to go to bed too, but their bedtime is just a bit later.'

'Yes, we do. But I didn't hold on to you tightly enough and you slipped out of my arms and broke some of your little bones. I'm really sorry mate.' I looked at Jade and could see the relief in her eyes. I knew she'd felt so terribly guilty since the night baby Charlie slipped out of her arms when she'd fallen asleep. The guilt was because she'd had two glasses of wine that night, the first since finding out she was pregnant all those months before. She hadn't realised how much they'd affect her. I shared some of the guilt, because I hadn't been as good to Jade as I should have been. I didn't get up in the middle of the night and pace round with Charlie over my shoulder, winding him or singing to him. I'd always rolled over and gone back to sleep.

'That's all right.' Charlie said, 'I quite like it. I'm like Nemo with a lucky fin.'

The bell rang and they stood up, Charlie began putting his jacket on.

'I'll bring him next time then.' Jade said, looking straight at me, nodding her head ever so slightly.

'Thanks.' I managed, struggling to keep it together.

'Bye Daddy.' Charlie said and waved as he walked away.

'Bye son.' I called after him. And to myself, not for the first time I prayed that he wouldn't turn out like me. Or his Uncle Aaron. A Peacock. For goodness' sake. What an idiot.

The Best Thing About Dying (Daniella's Tale)

You don't have to worry about other people anymore, when you're dying. You can do exactly what you like. And that includes not worrying what they think of you. It just doesn't matter as you're not going to be around long enough to care. Some people even think it's not your fault, it's the stress and the medication that's making you tetchy and they make allowances. Truth be told though, I have never spent much time worrying about what anyone else thinks of me. At my last appraisal, my manager said I wasn't exactly a people person, whatever that's supposed to mean. I like some people, and some people like me. It's just there aren't very many of them. Well, that's because long ago I stopped trying to behave how I was expected to and instead mostly did what I wanted, but with a little bit of reining myself in. Now, I didn't have to do any of that, and it was so liberating.

I find society quite perplexing and am inclined to think that if people were honest they'd admit they were only looking out for their own interests. Making friends and doing kind deeds is really only storing up favours and good karma for the future, in case you fall on hard times.

Josh said my outlook on life wasn't healthy. I tried to tell him that the less you mix with people, the fewer germs you'll catch, so surely that was healthy. He just looked at me with that expression I had become used to seeing. It was a bit like pity. It was certainly the one he wore when he watched news on the TV about flood and famine victims, or refugees fleeing their homes under gunfire. He clearly felt sorry for them. But he didn't need to feel sorry for me, I was perfectly happy. If I don't rely on other people, they can't let me down.

Over the eight months we were together, he tried several times to find a reason for what he described as my bitter view of the human race. When we were lying in bed together in the dark, after sex but before we drifted off to sleep, he'd cuddle me and ask about my childhood. I wracked my brains for images or memories of bad treatment from my parents or teachers or fellow students. But I just couldn't come up with anything. I did manage to recall that I'd asked for a bike one Christmas, which I didn't get. I must have been about seven. Josh drew his arm around me as I started to describe this bright shiny pink one I'd seen in the shop window, with tassels from the handlebars. He was clearly gearing himself up to console me as I felt him draw his hand tighter around my shoulder. It was as if he was all expectant, that he'd finally know the trigger to my cynical and uncaring disposition. Then I felt his arm withdraw and him roll over, saying he was tired when I finished the story, telling him I did get the bike, but not for two more months until it was my birthday and that for Christmas the present I got was the life-size talking, singing Amy doll that I'd also asked for.

By the time I left him, he'd stopped asking. I think he'd come to the conclusion that I was just like this, and no-one was to blame. When I say I left him, that's not strictly true. We'd had one of our regular arguments, following on from a night out at the pub with his mates. He'd accused me of being downright rude to his old school-friend Kai, about his wife. I'd said it wasn't my fault he didn't like her being called an alcoholic and if he didn't like it, he should try harder to keep her away from the booze. That was our last night together. He'd gathered his clothes and stormed out of the flat. He came back the next day when I was at work and took his half of the CD collection and a few other bits he'd brought with him when he'd moved in with me.

So the argument night was the last time I saw him. Well, saw him up close that is as I don't think you can really count watching him from across the road from his office or following a few paces behind him when he walked home to his mum and dad's house. I never liked them. They were nice enough to me at the start, but his mother in particular seemed to be against us being together and I distinctly heard her telling him in the kitchen one day, when she thought I was in the other room, that he deserved better. It got harder to see him once the injunction had been granted. The courts are so quick to issue them, even when you do the smallest amount of stalking.

I have wondered at length why I persisted in trying to see him. I think it's because he's the only person whose company I actually liked being in. And the more he didn't want to see me, the more I was determined to change his mind. And now I was dying, well that little legal piece of paper shouldn't matter. And since I'd resigned from my tedious job at the hardware shop, I had time on my hands to be with him. I suppose resign isn't the most accurate word to describe what happened. My manager said they'd had too many complaints to keep me on, the final one from the old lady that I'd told was probably better off without her late husband, now she'd discovered he'd had lots of debts.

I thought the best thing to do was just turn up at Josh's office. He'd be less likely to call the police in front of his colleagues, certainly not before I'd made my announcement. And it couldn't have gone better. There were at least ten people there when I arrived and I went straight up to him.

'Oh Josh,' I said, 'Thank goodness you're here. I didn't know who else to turn to. I've just had the most dreadful news. I've only got weeks to live.' And then I burst into tears, which I was quite pleased I was able to manage, since I very rarely shed any for real. Everyone rushed around me, one pulling a chair up and another thrusting a plastic cup of water in my hand. Someone else put their hand on my shoulder. A clean tissue was offered to me and I smiled at the benefactor with what I hoped was a sad expression. It was clear that Josh hadn't told any of his workmates about me and I'd never met any of them before, so they took me at my word. Another chair was pushed next to me and Josh guided into it, with a cup of water thrust into his hand too.

'What is it you've got?' a woman at the back of the group asked.

'Cancer,' I replied, suddenly realising I should have done some research.

'But you don't usually die from it these days,' another one piped up, 'my brother had chemo and radiotherapy and he's right as rain now.'

A male voice then added, 'not if it's a secondary one, they can't seem to get them sorted. They're the ones that still kill you.' After a pause he added, 'sorry, that didn't come out right.'

I found myself saying, 'That's what they said I had. That's why I've only got weeks. I didn't know I had it, but now I'm riddled with it.' I managed another cry and a cup of tea was offered, with lots of sugar.

Josh moved back in with me and became the most attentive boyfriend anyone could wish for. Now, when I'm cross with anyone, such as the time the cashier at the corner shop took forever to run my few items through the till, I tell them exactly what I think. I'm as rude as I like and Josh doesn't say a word. That's definitely the best bit. That I can be myself, say what I really think and he just accepts it. After all, I haven't got long.

I do struggle remembering what symptoms I'm supposed to have and I had to get a ton of innocuous tablets from health food shops, to keep up the pretence of taking a cocktail of life-prolonging, pain-relieving drugs. I told him I didn't want him coming to any appointments with me, because I was braver on my own. I explained that when he was with me, he took the strain off me and then I'd crumble, at the very time I needed to stay strong. I sometimes catch Josh looking at me as if he's wondering what I'm thinking. He asks a lot of questions and I try to be non-specific to avoid getting caught out. My reserve phrase for when he's getting too pushy, is that it upsets me to talk about it and I want to live what little time I have left, as carefree as possible.

I decided I'd also make sure he stayed with me by playing on his sense of duty. I was very convincing, I thought, on how frightened I was about dying alone in a hospital bed, in agony. He did however have a strange expression on him when he said he'd make sure that didn't happen. He must mean he'd make sure I had enough morphine and that he'd be right by my side, holding my hand.

I didn't have much of a plan, except that I would say I have periods where I was in remission and then it was getting hold of me again. Every time Josh asked if I wanted to find another job, or do some volunteering to get out and about more, luckily I felt poorly again, so he stopped making these suggestions. It was therefore quite a surprise when he said we should go on holiday. I was delighted, but said I didn't want to go abroad as it would make getting travel insurance quite complicated.

So here I am, enjoying some rare Scottish sunshine, bobbing around in an inflatable dinghy on a beautiful lake. We've had a lovely picnic and I have definitely drunk more wine than I usually did in the middle of the day. But I was thirsty from the salty gammon that Josh had put in the sandwiches and well, I wasn't driving so it didn't really matter. The decision to come to this area so far off the beaten track, had been his idea and as I'd never been to Scotland before, I was quite keen. We just camped in fields whenever we'd had enough of driving, it was so peaceful and so much wide-open space, you could go for hours without seeing anyone. Where we were now was particularly isolated, there didn't even seem to be any sheep or cattle, certainly no buildings.

It seemed a long time that Josh had been rowing and so I asked him if he was getting tired as I didn't mind if we didn't go any further.

'Yes,' he answered, 'I am tired. Tired of it all.' And that's when he stood up.

'Careful, you're making it rock.'

'Oh dear,' he said, but not in his normal, kind voice. In fact he sounded rather like me. Without warning he jumped over the side and made an almighty splash. He swam back to the side of the dinghy and began pulling it down before releasing it to rock back.

'Hey, stop it,' I said as I desperately clung to the ropes around the sides. 'This isn't funny.' I stood up to look at him and see if he was laughing. But he wasn't and instead of steadying it, he used all his strength to pull on one side again, making the boat capsize. I was so surprised I didn't have time to hold onto anything.

The water was freezing and immediately I started thrashing my arms around, desperately trying to keep my head above water. 'Josh, help me,' I called out, gasping for breath as I spat out some of the lake water that had washed towards me. 'I can't swim.'

'I know,' he answered as I watched him swim back towards the shore, dragging the dinghy behind him.

Even in my state of panic, I still wondered if maybe Josh was thinking this was a better end for me, than being in hospital. But if that was the case, why has he left me instead of comforting me? I called out his name, crossly at first then I changed to pleading or what I thought would sound most like that. Surely he hadn't worked out I was lying all along. Surely he'd realise his mistake and come back for me. My arms grew tired as I splashed around and kicked without any effect. My last thoughts are, whatever have I done to deserve this?

An Eye for an Eye *(Tony's Tale)*

The whisky splashed onto the kitchen table, as Tony refilled his glass. He drank it straight down, then picked the bottle up again and drained it.

'Who's drunk all my scotch?' he asked the empty house, his words slurred. Angrily he threw the empty bottle against the wall and stared at the pieces of broken glass scattered on the floor. He drank the dregs then pushed his glass away, it stopped close to the edge, next to an empty packet of cigarettes. He cradled his head in his arms on the table and was almost immediately asleep, snoring loudly.

The knocking on the door woke him just after eleven o'clock the next morning. He lifted his thumping head and blinked at the bright sunlight pouring in through the open curtains.

'Go away,' he shouted and rubbed the palms of his hands into his eyes. The knocking continued, it was the sound of a clenched fist beating, not the metallic tapping of the brass knocker. He could make out a man's voice bellowing to let him in, but it took a few seconds to recognise who it was.

'All right, all right, I'm coming.' He rose unsteadily to his feet and shuffled slowly over to the door.

'You took your time,' Mick said and strode into the kitchen without waiting for an invitation. 'Look at the state of this place.' He went into the living room but stayed standing, fidgeting with the corner of the newspaper he carried under his arm.

'Sit down Mick,' Tony said pointing at the armchair as he sat himself down on the sofa. Mick hesitated but then perched on the edge of the chair he had been directed to.

'This isn't exactly a social call. I came to, well …' his voice faltered, and then gaining strength, he continued, 'to find out how you could do such a thing.'

'What are you on about Mick?' Tony asked, looking him straight in the eye.

'This is what I'm on about,' he replied and thumped the newspaper down on the sofa.

Tony read the headline that'd been circled in pen. 'Bedford man stabbed to death in vicious attack,' he looked up, 'so?' He slumped back into his seat, folding his arms.

'It's not just any Bedford man, is it? It's Nicholas Taylor. Are you trying to tell me you don't remember him?'

'How dare you, of course I do. I couldn't forget the man who murdered my wife.' Tony was on his feet now.

'How many times do you have to be told? The jury acquitted him. It wasn't his fault she died.'

'Of course it was, he was driving the car. He was the one who ran over her. My Janet.' Tony's voice trailed off.

'So you killed him, in cold blood, is that what you did? To avenge her death.'

'No I did not. And it's got nothing to do with you. Anyway, the police have already been 'round. And they're quite satisfied with my whereabouts at the time he died. In case you want to check it out for yourself I was in The Golden Bell all evening, right up until closing time. I've got a pub full of alibis.'

Mick was bewildered for a moment, unsure if his first instinct was correct after all. But then he spoke with conviction. 'If it wasn't you personally, I bet you had something to do with it. You've had such hate in you since she died, I can't believe it was a coincidence. 'Go on, admit it, it was you wasn't it?' He was standing now, shouting down into Tony's face. 'It was, I know it was.'

The room was silent for a full minute before Tony finally replied. His voice was low and quiet. 'All right. It wasn't me personally. I paid some drug addict to do it for me. It was pathetic, he didn't care about what he was being paid to do, he was just so desperate for his next fix he'd do anything for the money. Half up front and half when the job's done. They'll never trace him, you see there's no connection, not between him and Taylor, or between him and me. It will simply go down as one of those unsolved cases.'

'But why?' Mick asked.

'You know why, because he killed Janet.'

'It wasn't his fault, you know that, you must do. He was found not guilty of death by dangerous driving. He wasn't even guilty of driving recklessly. It was dark, the roads were wet. She just stepped in front of him without looking, whilst she was talking on her phone.'

'I know she was on her phone. She was talking to me. I heard it all. The thump of her hitting the car. Her scream, him asking her if she was all right. Him calling the ambulance. All the while I was calling her name, I begged her to reply, to say something, but she couldn't because he'd killed her. So he had to die. An eye for an eye, a tooth for a tooth. His life for hers.'

'But it happened five years ago. Why now?'

'I couldn't find him until now, he's moved back into the area. Anyway, it doesn't feel like it happened five years ago, more like five minutes. My beautiful Janet. I still lay awake thinking about her night after night. I dream about her, about us being together, her laughing and smiling. We were so happy it just wasn't fair. I had to do something.' His voice was raised again. He sat down, resting his head in his hands. After a moment he looked at Mick. 'Are you going to tell the police then?'

'No. Whatever you've done, you're still my friend. I couldn't do that to you. I think you've punished yourself enough over the whole business. I don't think locking you up would do any good.'

'Thanks.'

Mick walked over to the door and without looking back, let himself out.

Tony sank into the armchair and read the newspaper article again, but this time slowly, savouring the news. He waited for it to take full effect, for him to feel relief that it was finally over. But he didn't, he felt the same as before, empty and longing for Janet. The knowledge that he'd planned it out so carefully, chosen someone unrelated and the murder had been carried out, gave him no comfort. Where was the relief he'd longed for? Why didn't he feel any better? He screwed the newspaper up and threw it to across the floor in disgust.

The alarm went off on his phone and he knew he'd have to hurry now to meet his contact at the agreed time. He took the bundle of twenty-pound notes from the kitchen drawer and left to meet the man he'd hired, to hand over the second half. He'd paid more than he'd intended as he'd convinced the addict to use a zombie knife, to look like a gang had done it. He hadn't noticed if the newspaper said that type of knife was used or not, they usually did. He knew this was not the type of transaction to quibble over not getting exactly what he'd paid for.

The payment was handed over and the addict ran away without a backward glance. Tony didn't know a man in a burgundy hoodie had watched from across the road.

Sean went straight to his sister's flat. He took the burgundy hoodie off and draped it over a dining chair.

'How did you get on?' Suzie asked. 'You must be frozen standing around all that time. Let me get you a coffee to warm you up.'

'Thanks sis.'

'Well did he go out?' she asked as she filled the kettle.

'Oh yes, he went out. He had a visit first though, from someone who wasn't happy with him, judging by the way they knocked on his door. He had a newspaper under his arm. Delaney took his time answering the door and he looked really rough. Not pleased to see this bloke either, but he did let him inside. Was there for about ten minutes.'

'Do you think this guy was involved in killing our Nicholas?'

'No, I think he was cross with Tony Delaney. Like us, he knew Tony was behind Nicholas's death.'

'We know Tony was in the pub all night. We know he didn't do it, but we also know Nicholas is dead, right after he comes back here, to a place where he's been threatened. And in the courtroom too, before the security guards got him. Not before he'd sworn he would kill Nicholas if he ever saw him again.'

'I know,' Sean answered, 'that's why Nicholas left in the first place and we both warned him not to come back. There are plenty of other places to live.'

'He wanted to be near us. He said he missed us.' Suzie put the coffee down in front of him.

'Thanks,' he warmed his hands on the cup. 'High price to pay though.'

'Where did Delaney go to today then?'

'He met a guy in an alleyway. Handed a bundle of money over to him.'

'Oh my God, so you saw the person who actually killed Nicholas!'

'Not clearly, he ran off. He was ever so skinny and really gaunt. Looked like a heroin addict. He just did it for the money I'm sure of it.'

'Do you want to ring the police and describe him to them?' She chewed at her thumbnail.

'No. It's not him I blame. It's Delaney.'

'Me too. So what are we going to do about Delaney then? The police won't do anything to him as he's got alibis. We'll have to get justice ourselves.'

'I'll sort it. I've been following him for days now. I know where he goes, including the backstreets that aren't well lit and no cameras around. I think it's time for a fatal mugging.'

'I hope Nicholas can rest in peace then.'

'He will sis, you leave it to me.'

The Tea Service *(Edith's Tale)*

I had even more than she did. So naturally I thought, well, it was Malcolm really, he thought, that it would be worth even more than she'd got. She only had a teapot and I had a lot more. Nearly all of it.

It was famous that episode, the one with the teapot. I know it was a long time ago, must be late 1980s or 1990s maybe, but it was shown again on one of those highlight programmes, where the experts reminisce about their favourite antiques and the funny people they've met. I think it was David someone who was telling the tale about it. This lady, she seemed ever so nice, owned this rare teapot and in the original programme he said it was worth quite a bit of money. And in the highlights programme, he said that she told them later how she'd sold it at auction and it had gone for such a lot, she'd been able to buy her council house with the money. He was ever so chuffed for her.

Malcolm saw the programme, same as I did. He told me that I should see about getting my tea set looked at maybe at a local auction house. He said it should be worth even more than the woman on the telly got, because I'd got the whole lot. I didn't say that one of the cups had been broken, because he didn't like to be reminded of that incident. He'd got the service out, when he knew he shouldn't have done. Said he was having a teddy bear's picnic. I thought he was a bit old for that, at ten, and he didn't like bears anyway, it was all Action Man, but I didn't want to tell him off for playing an innocent little game. But he got a bit cross when I asked him to put it away. It broke ever so easily. He said he was sorry. Like he always did.

I still like watching all the antiques programmes. And only recently, there was a woman with a teapot that belonged to Admiral Nelson. That was worth £20,000. So Malcolm could be right, the set could be worth a whole lot more than that.

When Malcolm heard that the Roadshow was coming near here, he was adamant that I should take the tea service to it. He said I could do the same as that other woman and buy my council house. I laughed and said it would never be enough for that, but he told me not to worry, he'd pay the rest, as he could borrow it. He said he just needed a big deposit and then he could come and live here with me, to keep me company. I have been lonely sometimes since Malcolm left home. He lived with a girl for years before she threw him out. Then he moved in with another one, then another. He's already hinted things aren't going well with this latest. I'm not really surprised. Malcolm is difficult to get on with. He has his ways of doing things and he just gets a bit worked up if you don't follow what he's said.

My poor husband, George, he died when Malcolm was only tiny. He had cancer and was in such terrible pain at the end. I didn't find the right man after that, not that was right for me and Malcolm, someone that could love us both. When he was a teenager, life was difficult for us. It wasn't his fault, what with all those hormones rushing through him at that stage of life. And the teachers didn't help the situation, being too rigid with homework and telling him when he had to get it in by. He said he wasn't going to be told what to do and he left as soon as he could. I was so pleased he got a job with an electrician. Somehow he found the patience to listen to what he was told and stick with it. Got his qualifications so he's his own boss now. He likes that.

I remember how quiet it was in those first months when he left. And how much I started to like living on my own. I wasn't so on edge. But that feeling returns, whenever he does. I don't want to upset him by saying the wrong thing. His new proposal to live here again full time, if I bought it, was unexpected. I wasn't sure it was the right thing to do at all. I said he shouldn't have to move in with me, he's got his own life now, he ought to be with his young friends, not his old mother. But he said he wanted to, and that it was the only way he'd get on the property ladder, since houses were going up all the time.

I'm not sure how easy it would be for him to get a mortgage, being self-employed, but he said he'd looked online and there were specialist lenders. Well, if Malcolm can't borrow enough, I wouldn't be the one stopping his big plan. So he shouldn't blame me at least.

He's a good boy, my Malcolm. He works hard, but he hasn't had a lot of luck finding work that really suits him. I'd love him to settle down with a nice girl, have a couple of grandchildren for me to spoil.

I knew the tea service had to be valuable, that's why it was always put away in the cupboard. It only came out on special occasions. I got it when my Mum died, who had it passed down from her Mum, my Granny Maud. Maud had worked in service, and at her last job, the mistress of the house left the tea service to her, for being such a loyal servant and companion. That's exactly how it was written in the will, a loyal servant and companion. The old lady hadn't got any family, and she took a shine to my Granny Maud. The old lady told her that it had been in her family for four generations and it was French.

I began to think Malcolm could be right, that it could be worth thousands. I wouldn't have thought of using the money to buy the house with, even though that's what the teapot lady did. Mind you I don't know what I'd spend thousands of pounds on. I think I'm a bit too old to go travelling or whatever they do these days. Malcolm says putting money in houses is the best thing. He said if you own a property, you can always rent it out especially one as big as this, and that would bring in loads of cash. I asked him where we'd live if we rented it out, but he said we wouldn't need to worry, we'd be rolling in it and could live where we liked. I said I liked it here best. I've got the garden all nice now, those seeds I planted will be coming up this year. Of course I can't do as much as I used to. And since I had the accident and hurt my hip, it's more difficult to bend down. Malcolm said it would make sense to live where there was a smaller garden. Maybe he's got a point.

I expect these Roadshow people have seen the same stuff hundreds of times, but they didn't show it. I'd thought I could just take a couple of plates down, and the teapot as well, but Malcolm said they wouldn't get the full picture unless they saw the lot. He lent me one of his suitcases on wheels, that he'd taken to Tenerife. So I filled it up with the teapot, milk jug, sugar bowl, 4 plates, 4 saucers and 3 cups. I wrapped them up really carefully, as I didn't want to risk them getting broken, especially as I had to get it on and off the bus. But it was all right in there, all safe and sound. I'd asked Malcolm if he could drive me there, but he was up against a deadline, he'd said. Never mind, the bus went quite close to the mansion house it was being held at.

    I told my next-door neighbour, Brian, all about going there. He was really pleased for me. I didn't tell him what I might use the money for though, Malcolm doesn't like me discussing family matters with others. Ever such a nice chap is Brian. He's a builder and he's always helping me out, if I've got something heavy to lift or need a hand fixing something. He knows Malcolm's very busy and he says he doesn't mind. He offered to give me a lift to the show, but I couldn't impose on him, so I said I'd got transport all sorted. Well I had, it was the number 43 I needed from the High Street.

    My friend Lydia would love to have come with me, she loves old things. But she's having trouble with her bunions and can't walk too far, so I went on my own.

    I think the chap I saw was called Trevor, or was it Thomas? I'm not sure now. It seemed like forever that I was in that queue. But that suitcase was a blessing, I only had to nudge it a bit and it rolled along on those wheels in each corner. Mind you, I did feel bad when I knocked into a couple of people's ankles, when I got a bit too-swift with it. He was ever so nice, Trevor or Thomas. He was very patient while I got it all out and spread it on the table. He said there was a small chip on one of the plates, and of course, he noticed there was a cup missing. He said if it had been a complete set and in perfect condition it would have been worth a bit more, but not much.

    I stood there, waiting for the verdict. It was like I was on trial or something. Such a lot could change, just because of how much the service was worth. I knew how pleased Malcolm would be if he could buy the house with me. Then Trevor or Thomas finally said this was a fine example of a mid-Victorian tea service by someone or other, but I didn't really hear him. It was very rude of me, but I jumped straight in and told him, sorry, but he was mistaken. It was French, and at least five generations old. That couldn't be mid Victorian. He smiled at me and asked if that's what I'd been told. I said yes and explained all about Granny Maud being a loyal servant and companion. He kept smiling and said what a nice gift that she'd received, but it definitely wasn't what she had been told. He turned the plate upside down and pointed to things painted on it. He said how it proved it was by, I don't know, someone or other and that their work was at its height in 18-something. I was stunned. Poor Granny Maud had been duped, and Mum and now me. The nice expert said it was a lovely piece. I hardly dared ask how much it was worth, but he told me without having to. About £800 he said. Then all I could think of was that I couldn't buy my house and a flood of relief washed over me. I hadn't wanted to rent it and move out. Or permanently share it with Malcolm for that matter.

But then I pictured Malcolm's face when I told him. I packed the tea service away as quickly as I could, I knew they were waiting to talk to the next person in the queue. I missed my bus and had to wait another hour for the next one. Still, it gave me time to think. Malcolm said he was going to come round at teatime, to see how I got on. I wondered what Brian was doing for his tea. I could invite him round for a bite to eat perhaps. He'd once said to me he wouldn't mind coming round, if I needed moral support at all. He had a strange expression on his face when he said it. I thought maybe the sun was in his eyes, as we were in the garden at the time.

He once said the walls were really quite thin. At first I thought he meant there was a structural problem which he knew about because he was a builder. Then I realised he was being discreet. I think he was at home when Malcolm and I had words. We often did, when he came to visit and especially if he stayed for a few days. Nothing I did was ever right for him, and he didn't hold back on telling me. It's this generation, they don't have the respect that mine did. I'd never have spoken to my parents like that. And certainly not anything more. I'm sure some men just don't know their own strength. It's my own fault, I should put a bit more meat on my bones and then I'd have a bit of padding if I bumped into something. Or get knocked over. I do think Brian might enjoy a bit of tea. Maybe some bacon and eggs; builders like that. I decided I'd definitely ask him to come round. Then I can break the news to Malcolm that we won't be able to buy the house after all.

After that evening, when Malcolm got so worked up, he didn't visit for quite some time. He'd been so mad at me and I was so glad to have Brian there. Malcolm said I couldn't have explained the history of the tea service properly and that if I had, they would have seen it was French. Brian was ever so good. He just stood up. Didn't say anything, and then, ever so quietly, said I wasn't to blame for it not being valuable. Malcolm didn't like that and left in a bit of a huff. Forgot his key as he rushed out. I decided not to give it back to him. So now, if Malcolm wants to come round, he tells me when and Brian joins us for a spot of tea. It works out very well. I still see him quite often. He asks to borrow a few pounds here and there and it's never more than I can afford. So I'm all right with that. I've got myself a little dog now, Milo. Malcolm doesn't like dogs, but I do.

Accidental Death *(Will's Tale)*

Will was slouched in the armchair with his feet resting on the coffee table. He'd polished off half a can of beer in the ten minutes since he'd sat down to watch the match on TV. He didn't care that crisp crumbs were leaking onto his seat from the grab bag he'd got from the cupboard and started eating before he'd even sat down. He heard a car pull up outside and footsteps running down the path. He was annoyed his solitude had been interrupted and took his feet down. He'd been enjoying being at home without the rest of the family being there. With five of them living together, it was rare for him to have such peace. He'd turned down the offer to go to the cinema with his dad and sisters, he'd rather see the film with his mates. And Mum was seeing her friend who'd just come out of hospital. She'd be gone ages, as once she got talking there was no stopping her.

    He was retrieving some crumbs when he looked up to see his mum standing in front of him. Rain dripped from her red coat and her wet hair was plastered to the sides of her face. But it was her expression that disturbed him. He noticed she was shaking.

    'Mum, whatever's the matter?'

    'I think I killed him.'

    'What?' he leapt out of the chair and went over to her, holding her freezing cold hands. 'What do you mean you think you killed him?'

    'Don't shout at me Will. It wasn't my fault.' Her voice trembled and tears poured down her face.

    'Sorry, look let me take this off and sit down.' He pulled her coat off her, threw it over the chair and sat next to her.

    'Did you call an ambulance? Should we ring them now?' He got his mobile out of his pocket.

    'No.' She shook her head, 'no.'

    'Well what happened?'

    She reached into her pocket and brought out a crumpled tissue and blew her nose. She took a deep breath. 'I couldn't help it, he just ran in front of me.'

    'In front of the car you mean, where?'

'Yes, in Cavendish Road. I tried to stop in time, but you see what it's like out there, it's been raining all day. The roads are so wet, I braked as soon as I could, but I skidded into him and heard this loud thud!' Her voice was high and she was almost hysterical,

'Calm down Mum, it was an accident.' He put his arm around her back to try and comfort her. He tried to appear much calmer than he felt. The thought of his mum on trial and even going to prison was disturbing, she'd never cope.

'What makes it worse, you see, is that I sort of knew him. Well I'd seen him around, you know, recognised him.'

'Who was he?' Will asked.

'I don't know his name, or where he lives, I'd just seen him, out and about.'

'Did you stop and look at him properly, maybe he's only stunned, just unconscious.' He looked hopeful.

'Yes I stopped. He was dead, he was so still and there was blood all over the road.' She started sobbing again.

'Did you try and find out his name?'

'Oh no, I couldn't get that close, it was too horrible. What's everyone going to think of me? I didn't mean to do it, you must believe me. You do don't you?'

'Yes of course I do. People will understand I'm sure.' He tried to sound convincing.

'Maybe they won't find out, what do you think? We don't have to tell anyone do we Will?' She looked straight at him with her green eyes, pleadingly.

'Well I don't know, what about the police?' He chewed his bottom lip nervously. 'They might have seen your car on CCTV or the neighbour's cameras, you know on their doorbells.'

'Yes, they'll find out it was me.'

'Look, perhaps we should go back and see if he really is dead first. Then we'll know where we stand.'

'OK Will, if you think that's best. But I can't drive, not now. You'll have to.' She held her hand out to him with the keys resting on the upturned palm.

He took them and was about to say that they didn't have any L plates for that car but decided it didn't matter under the circumstances. Pulling the door shut behind him, he unlocked the old, but reliable, Renault. They ran across in the rain and he squeezed into the driver's seat, groping for the lever to move the seat back.

'Don't worry, it'll be all right,' he said trying to sound as he had the situation under control. But he hadn't had many lessons and he'd never driven in rain this heavy before. He drove slowly, but even so he could see his mum was startled by the noise of the car going through a deep puddle, throwing up spray high enough to reach her window. He hadn't expected the steering wheel to jerk to the left, from the force of driving through it either.

'How far along is it?' He asked when they turned into Cavendish Road.

'I think it was a bit further up.' She was sobbing again, groping for a tissue, but not finding one.

'OK. It'll be fine, you'll see.' He felt as if he'd turned into the parent, trying to reassure his child.

'Stop, stop!' she screamed,

He slammed on the brakes, surprised at how long it took to completely stop on the wet road. They both got out of the car. Will started to feel sick, he'd never seen a dead body and didn't know what to expect when he saw one. He felt his heart racing as he went over to where his mum was standing. 'Here he is,' his mother whispered.

He stared down to where she pointed. He couldn't believe what he was seeing. After a moment he looked at her confused. 'That's a cat. You said you ran someone over.'

'Is he definitely dead Will?' She'd bent down but her hand was still not touching him.

'Let me see.' He squatted next to her and felt the cat's neck. It was hard to tell as the black and white fur was long and sodden with the rain. 'I think so.'

'Oh no. Feel again, maybe we should take him to a vet.' She stood back.

Will wanted to help his mum get over this, as she was obviously so distressed, but he couldn't help feeling relief. It was only a cat, he almost laughed. Of course, his mum hadn't run a man over and just left him there. It all made sense now. He felt round its neck.

'A vet can't help him now. He's gone and there's no collar, so I don't know who he belongs to. Did you see him outside a particular house, we could knock on their door.'

'No, just along this road at different places.'

'Look, let's leave him on the pavement and when his owner comes looking for him, at least he'll know what's happened to him.'

'That's not a very nice way to find out.'

'No maybe not. But we could come back in the morning and maybe ask around then.' He was keen to get home now. The match would be well underway, and he thought his mum would just go up to bed.

'All right. Thanks Will, I don't know what I'd have done without you.' She squeezed his hand and got back in the car.

Will lifted the cat onto the pavement and wiped his hands dry on his jeans. As he drove back, he felt pleased with how he'd managed to help out and his dad would surely lighten up towards him, when he heard. Dad had been critical lately of his lack of success in getting a job, but he was trying, a bit. Enough to keep the Jobcentre happy. He'd got an interview lined up at a warehouse that had just opened on the industrial estate, so he'd might be able to pay his way, fairly soon. He wanted to cheer his mum up. She often came to his defence when Dad was having a rant.

'At least he died quickly. He wouldn't have suffered.' He said.

'I do hope not.' She managed to blow her nose on half a tissue she's pulled out of her trouser pocket. Her crying had at last ceased.

'I didn't tell you earlier, I've got an interview on Wednesday, at that warehouse.'

'That's wonderful, I hope it goes well.' She smiled at him.

'I'll cycle up there to start with until I've passed my test. Might get an electric bike. That'll be good.' He was enthusiastic about that. It was a bit uphill coming home and he didn't like pedalling up hills. He was just about to ask for some money to buy one and pay her back when he got his first lot of wages, when his mum screamed.

'Stop, stop!'

It was too late. The car slowed as he slammed his foot on the brake, but it continued on the wet road, long after he needed it to stop. After he'd knocked over the man in dark clothing, who'd been hurrying along in the rain, walking his dog.

Me and Mr G *(Jason's Tale)*

I've always been good with computers and using the internet is something I do particularly well. I don't need any of this artificial intelligence, I've got enough of my own. That's all anyone talks about is this AI, but that's because they don't know what I know, which is how the internet works. That's why I can't get a job in IT, because I'd show everyone else up with how good my skills are. That and the complete short-sightedness of some employers who want qualifications and experience in a workplace. They don't appreciate that what you can learn yourself, is just as important. Well it's their loss. I'd make a perfectly good employee for the right company, for someone who can see just what I can do. He's my mate, you see, Mr G. Or Mr Google if I'm feeling a bit more formal with him. Ask him anything and there it all is.

Mum and Dad had been good about my situation I suppose. They've stopped nagging me now to find work and finally realise that I have very good reason for not being in a remunerative position, which is that I've not being treated right. Obviously I have to ask for cash for things from time to time because the stingy government won't pay me any benefits anymore because I won't go after just any old job. Luckily Mum's eyesight's too bad for her to drive now. So they need me to ferry them to the shops and the endless hospital visits. I don't ever want to get old, I'd rather someone shot me while I still had some dignity. I might do it myself. I certainly wouldn't be moaning all day about how expensive everything is these days and how long the wait is to see a doctor or get an appointment at one clinic or another. It's her car, so it's only right she pays to tax and insure it. I use her debit card to put the petrol in, but of course she's using most of it with my taxi-service. Dad keeps threatening to drive it himself, but Mum says he mustn't because of his funny turns. I don't know what they'd do without me. So I help them stay independent, by not doing too much for them. Otherwise, when the right company comes along that wants me to work for them, well then they'd really struggle.

If they'd been a bit more generous with me, I wouldn't have been in this predicament. Sometimes I think I'm just so unlucky. That's the way it's been with my last two girlfriends. I wasn't really over the first one, Honesty, when I met the second, but when you're in love, what can you do?

Honesty was the most beautiful woman I'd ever seen. We talked for hours on Zoom and she told me all about her life in Nigeria. She'd never heard of the Billy Joel song "Honesty", and I'd sing a bit to her every time she logged on. She had a great laugh, really infectious. I'd been putting money aside for the airfare to go over and meet her, when the most awful thing happened. Her twin sister Grace was arrested by the police. It was because she's a journalist who was about to write an article exposing police corruption. Honesty was beside herself and I couldn't blame her, after all the conditions in Nigerian prisons can't be good. It was what she said they'd do to her, that really frightened Honesty.

I offered to fly out and see if I could talk some sense into them, but she said that they wouldn't listen to a foreigner. When I asked her what would help she couldn't stop crying and refused to say. It took me several hours before she finally told me there really was only way to get her out. And that, and here's the irony, was she'd have to pay a bribe. I said we'd have to do that then, after all we couldn't leave Grace in there to the mercy of those prison guards. All men. Honesty had shown me a picture of her sister and they really were identical. I couldn't stand by and let it go on, so I wired the money over as she requested.

She could only contact me once after that. She said it had worked exactly to plan and Grace was free, but now neither of them were safe. Because they looked alike, they were both going to have to move away and live under the radar. Which meant no more Zooming because the police would be tracking that. I knew she was right. Mr G confirmed there were all sorts of corruption and improper practices going on over there by police and government. I couldn't risk anything bad happening to her, so we said goodbye for good. She took her profile off the dating website and that was that. I was gutted but at least they were both safe, and if I left her alone, she would stay safe.

I was only looking around the web out of boredom one afternoon and then the picture of this beautiful Indonesian girl caught my eye. She was called Lin-Lin and everything about her was magical. We chatted for ages on Zoom and I felt quite guilty at times, that I'd found myself a new girlfriend, without having said goodbye to Honesty all that long ago. But Lin-Lin was very good and said she'd wait until I was ready. She even said she wouldn't answer my calls for a whole week to give me the time to sort my thoughts out, but I didn't need to do any sorting. I hadn't cheated on Honesty and I deserved some happiness. I just had to start saving up for an airfare again.

I asked Mum and Dad for an advance but Dad said no, what was there an advance of, only more handouts. Well he can walk to the chemist and get his own asthma inhalers next time, I thought. Mum got them for him in the end, he's such a lazy git. She gives me bits of money here and there when I asked for it. The big expenses like my broadband and mobile phone contracts, they were all on direct debit from their bank, so I didn't have to ask every month for those. Just for bits here and there for new clothes, going out with my mates and meals out and that sort of thing. My body building protein supplements cost quite a bit, but she can pay for that when she gets her cod liver oil tablets.

I was managing to put a bit of money to one side as I say, for the flight and it would all have been fine, if only she hadn't had the accident. Everyone knows how bad the roads are out there, Mr G has umpteen YouTube clips of tuk tuks weaving in and out of each other. Funnily enough, I'd only showed her a couple the previous week. Of course it wasn't funny at all, it was really serious and put her in the hospital. Now she said she's stable and they can send her home. But if she's to ever walk again, they need to do an operation in the next week or it'll be too late. I couldn't bear her stuck in a wheelchair, not when my gorgeous Lin-Lin was born to dance, and dance with me as soon as I could get over there.

So of course I asked my parents for the flight money. I thought they'd agree, well that Mum would at least, but no, not a penny. And I didn't have anywhere near enough. Mum said I should leave it to her family to sort her out and that I should find myself a nice local girl. I told her she was just being racist and that if she'd been English it would have been different. She tried to argue it wasn't that at all and that I didn't really know anything about her. This romance could all be some kind of scam, just like the last one. Well I said some things to her then I'm not very proud of, but I made my point it was no such thing and she was just a jealous old crone. I thought after that maybe I'd gone too far so I muttered that I was sorry at dinner and she seemed okay again.

Clearly, they weren't going to help out and I was really worried about Lin-Lin. There was no way I wasn't going to get that money for her. I knew it was pointless applying for a credit card or even a payday loan as I'd already gone through every company Mr G could find for me. So I had to use my wits to get the money. Normally I would regard myself as a good, law-abiding citizen but I had to make the difficult decision that Lin-Lin's needs were greater than my clean criminal record. And anyway, there's no reason I should get caught.

It was Mum mentioning scams that got me thinking. I used Mr G to give me some ideas and finally came up with a fool proof plan. Every year until they couldn't drive, they went to Weston-super-Mare and stayed in this cottage about five miles from the seafront. Mum loved it. She said it was cosy and secluded and had this big apple tree in the garden that they were allowed to pick fruit from. She said she really enjoyed baking crumbles and pies straight after picking the apples. And it was called Apple Tree Cottage, wasn't that quaint. Not really I'd thought and then she'd said that they never had to worry about forgetting the code to the key safe for the front door key, as it was the year I was born. Mr G showed me the webpage where it was advertised for rental, and I could see that checkout was on a Saturday morning at 10 a.m. and check-in wasn't until 4p.m. I remember Mum saying it was a rush to get packed and out, since the cleaner was always prompt as Apple Tree was the first on her list.

It was easy to register Apple Tree cottage on the Rent It Now! website, showing it available to rent for a six-monthly tenancy. No references required as a tenant was needed urgently because of moving abroad for work. I uploaded the cottage photos that I copied from the holiday website. I did a bit of a summary and took out bits about places of interest and put in that there were good local schools and transport links. That's what Mr G showed me on the rental websites. I made up a new Gmail account for email enquiries and only a few hours later my prospective tenant Harry, made contact. I told him I could see him at the property at 12.00 on Saturday and that I'd need a cash deposit of £1,000 if he wanted to secure it. I had other interested parties coming after him, so it would be whoever paid the deposit first. He sounded keen, telling me his girlfriend had just kicked him out and he was anxious to get sorted quickly so that his lad could still visit him. We agreed on midday. I was quite excited and drove down to get there in plenty of time. I watched the cleaner leave at half eleven and before long I'd retrieved the key from the safe, entering my year of birth. It was as if it was all meant to be.

I used the time to walk 'round the little cottage trying to anticipate what sort of questions a tenant might ask. I used my phone to look up more information about the area, including some local pub names. He rang the doorbell right on time and I showed him around my lovely home that I was so sad to be leaving. He asked me if I had the tenancy agreement he could sign as he was anxious to secure the property. He said he had the cash with him. I said of course, and produced a tenancy agreement that I'd copied from a website, with all the usual jargon on it, with Apple Tree Cottage's address. I'd been referring to myself by a different name, so I made sure I put that one down. It didn't matter that he'd signed a worthless piece of paper, but he looked relieved when he'd done it.

Harry handed me the money and in return I promised I'd cancel the other viewings. He went away happy with the keys in his hand. I was chuffed to bits I'd got the money to make Lin-Lin better. It was lucky medical care was relatively cheap out there. If it had been America, it would have been thousands.

  The knock at the door was the following day and it hadn't taken the police long once they'd met Mum and Dad, to know that they hadn't pulled off the almost-perfect crime. When I asked them how they found out, they said that Harry had been in touch after he'd had holiday guests turning up at the door, expecting to stay. With a bit of looking on the internet, he'd found the cottage advertised as a holiday rental. Yes, I said, all right, but how did you track it back to me? You gave him your phone number they said, just as they'd read me my rights. I want to use Mr G, I said, thinking I should find out a good defence strategy. They said there was plenty of time for me to call my solicitor. What idiots I thought but cursed them at the same time. I hadn't had a chance to get to the bank before it shut, so I knew they'd give Harry his money back. Poor Lin-Lin. Confined to a wheelchair for the rest of her life and all because I'd used my actual phone number. How could someone like me have made such a simple mistake?

Centre Stage *(Jack's Tale)*

I think that's the police coming. I can see some flashes of black and white uniforms, just when people in the crowd were getting really enthusiastic, clapping along to the catchy melody of one of my favourites. That summed up my luck. This could have been the day, the one time I'd get spotted by a talent scout. I mean that's what happened to Brian. Not that anyone knew him as that. His stage name was Blake Ivory.

I know I shouldn't have done it, but Blake was always so arrogant, he had it coming. Granted the fans came to hear him and we got great audiences wherever we toured, but he wasn't even playing his own music. Not like I did. I had the ideas, the guitar playing and the voice for it, whereas Blake basked off the back of other people's talent. Fair enough he had a great voice, and he was able to work the crowd, make his fans feel he was singing directly to them. And he could play the piano really well. That's why he'd chosen that surname. He was always on about tickling the ivories when he was practicing.

There were six of us in the band, including Blake. He did the usual at some point during the performances, of introducing us one by one. We stepped forward and did a little solo instrumental bit, which the audience always liked. Last year he'd let me sing a song I had written, as it was my twenty-first birthday. It was amazing and it went down really well. I asked him if I could sing regularly, but he'd given me a look as if I should know my place.

'Don't get ahead of yourself lad, it's still me they're coming to see.' He'd said.

'Of course Blake. I just thought it would add something to the show. They loved it when I sang on my birthday.'

'Well it was good of me to let you. I didn't expect to be rewarded by you going on at me to repeat it. It was a one-off.'

'Sorry. It's your show, obviously. Would you have a look at the new song I've written? I think it would really suit your voice.' I asked, hungry from some crumbs from his plate.

'Sure, drop it into my dressing room.'

I should have known he'd only agreed to read it to shut me up. It wasn't completely true that it suited his voice. It suited mine better, someone young and fit, not middle-aged and pretty much past it, taking a nap in the afternoon whenever there was a chance. But that visit to his dressing room was where I got the idea from. He was already in there, humming away doing his vocal warm-ups. Suddenly it changed to shouting, with him say get off, get off. I rushed inside and there was a moth flying around. At first I didn't realise it was the moth that was bothering him, I thought there was someone I hadn't yet noticed.

'Kill it, quickly, get it,' he said as he pushed past me and left the room.

I managed to trap it in a glass and slide one of our advertising leaflets underneath. It went crazy, crashing into the glass at every turn. I didn't like to hurt it, so I thought I'd just release it outside. I walked past Blake and held the glass up.

'Got it,' I said, expecting his gratitude.

'Don't show it to me, you stupid idiot.' He barged past Jamie, our drummer and stormed off.

'What's got into him?' I asked.

'He's got a phobia about moths. You know like people have with spiders. Proper creeps him out,' Jamie replied. 'I better check he's okay.'

I looked down at the poor moth, still trying desperately to find an escape route. Sorry, I told him silently, I think I'm going to need you. I put the glass down carefully behind the stage where it wouldn't be noticed. We were at this venue for two shows, Blake having put his favourites into a two-part collection. The fans loved it, knowing they could see him twice and hear different songs each night. It was our fourth venue with this format, and it was great for us, having a night in the same place we were playing the next day. We actually had time to see the sights in daylight.

I went to the bar and picked up an empty glass with barely any drink left in it and one of the bar mats littered about. If there was one, maybe there would be another. I looked around, shaking curtains to see if anything had settled and not easy to spot. I put all the lights on I could and opened some more windows. I went into the gents and that's where I was rewarded. A moth was busy investigating the central light fitting.

Luckily I was tall, six foot four when I last measured and so I could reach without having to get a chair. The thing wasn't particularly easy to catch though, and I was worried someone would come in at any moment. If they did, I'd already thought I would say I was catching it before Blake saw it. Although it would have scuppered my plans, it would have given me some brownie points for looking out for the boss.

Eventually I caught it and put it next to the earlier one. This had slowed down to a half-hearted flutter every few seconds. I pictured them communicating with each other, the new one willing the other one to try harder to get out and the old one saying there was no point, they were done for. It gave me an idea for a song and I left to scribble down some notes about different perspectives for the same situation.

I asked Blake again if he'd thought about singing my new song, but he said it wasn't right for the show. It wasn't what the punters were expecting. I tried to argue that they loved new things, that he was always finding new songwriters' stuff, airing it for the first time. I wanted to add that he enjoyed taking the credit for a new discovery, when he was only doing the easy bit, but I held back, just in case he'd change his mind. When it was clear he wasn't going to, I knew I'd have to put my plan into action.

By the time we were due to go on for the second night, both moths were dead. I scooped them up in a tissue and gently folded it around them, trying hard not to crush them. I needed them to still look like moths. Blake would play the first half without music, he knew those ones so well, but the second half he wasn't so sure of, so he put out his music book.

That was my chance. In the interval, I sneaked back on stage, the audience oblivious to me being there, the other side of the curtain. I tipped both moths between the fourth and fifth pages. He'd have got long enough into the session that the audience would be having a great time. But not so close that the show would have to end, when he caught sight of them and had a panic. I could picture it as clearly as if I'd witnessed it already. He'd be freaked out when they floated towards him with the wind the turning page created. He'd cry out, just as he'd done in the dressing room and run away from the stage.

I would step forward, apologise for Blake having a problem, smooth things over and say here's something for them to listen to, until Blake comes back. I didn't need any of the band, I could just come forward, to centre stage and sing my brilliant new song.

The second half was going well and by the third piece the applause was really loud, with cheering too. I was nervous, aware that they were here for Blake and they might think me a poor substitute when I did my solo. I reassured myself they'd love it, they'd love me, just as they had on my birthday.

Blake turned to the fourth page of his music book. The moths were right on cue, seeming to fly out of the papers, straight into his face. He let out a scream, even more startled than I'd hoped. I looked down and tried to calm my nerves. I let the notes of the intro flow through my head and I closed my eyes whilst I tried to centre my concentration. I looked up, expecting to see Blake on his feet, halfway out of the door. He was standing, but staggering, grasping at his chest, his face contorted with pain. He looked up at me and our eyes met for a second. He knew I'd done this.

There was no stepping forward, launching my song onto a huge audience. Instead the house lights went up and the bass player shouted out is anyone a doctor? Blake had collapsed on the stage. The crowd was noisy, voicing concerns, asking if he was all right. Someone came forward and said they were a nurse and then were nudged out of the way by someone saying they were a consultant. Jamie said he was calling 999 and the doctor asked if there was a defibrillator in the building. Despite all the fussing around him, Blake died.

And the tour died too. I was out of work again and it had all gone horribly wrong. How I wish I could turn the clock back and just be happy being part of a great band. I still believe one day I will get my big break. I just need to be discovered, so I'm on social media, I have videos on TikTok and I play whenever I can, hoping I'll get noticed.

Now I seem to have been noticed by the police and so I grab my collection hat, folding stool and run off, before they tell me again that busking is illegal without a permit. As if I could afford one of those.

Seen through a Window *(Isaac's Tale)*

Isaac sat looking out of the window, from the ledge that wasn't really deep enough for him to be on anymore. He had homework to do, but he didn't like maths and so he'd leave it to the last possible minute. He was more likely to get some help with it if he only had a really short time to complete it. His mum and dad didn't like him not handing it in or submitting it late, so they explained it all to him as quickly as they could, virtually giving him the answers to just get it done.

He wished he could get their attention at other times. Mum liked to have a shower in the morning and if he went into the bathroom to ask her where he might have left something, he got shooed away. But she was in there ages as she had such long hair that it took her forever to get the shampoo out of it. He'd watched her sometimes before she realised he was there, but he'd only seen her from behind. He'd started to be curious about what she'd look like from the front, without anything on. After all she wouldn't look like he did, she had big boobs and no thingy.

He once saw, for the shortest moment, a picture on Dad's tablet, which was of some women with hardly any clothes on. He walked into his study where Dad worked from home and was looking over his shoulder, before Dad realised he was there. He'd never seen his dad move so fast before.

There was the time he went into his sister's room when she was getting dressed, but he was just a tiny bit too late. She'd put her top on and was just buttoning up her jeans. She was really rude to him and threw her pillow at him. Mum told him off for prying and then she had a lock put on the door.

It was a warm day and the window was open, but not very far. He didn't like the idea of going splat on the pavement, so he knew not to lean out. It was only a narrow road outside the house and then straight across there was a park with bushes around the outside. It was usually deserted, but he liked to watch out for dogs, and he was allowed to borrow Dad's binoculars as he'd promised to take care of them. He had a notebook where he wrote down the different breeds he saw. His favourites were Pugs and Dachshunds, and he caught sight of what he thought might be a miniature Dachshund. They were the absolute best. But when it got closer he could see it was just a terrier.

He was about to go downstairs and see if he could swipe a biscuit from the tin without anyone noticing, when he saw a couple of teenagers stop where there was a gap in the bushes. The boy leant down to kiss the girl, and she put her arms around his neck. Isaac looked around for the binoculars, eager to see more of what they were up to. He found them under his school jumper that he'd dropped on the floor. He looked through them and managed to get the couple into focus.

He watched as they took a step into the bushes together, the boy leading her by the hand. Isaac couldn't believe his luck when she unzipped her sweatshirt. This could be it, he might get to see them at it. He had no idea what that actually was but knew enough to think they'd be naked. And most importantly, that she would be naked. He leaned out as far as he dared, excited at what he might see.

He could hear her raised voice, and it sounded like she was saying no. He couldn't have been more disappointed as he watched the boy close his hands around the girl's neck. She struggled and kicked around until eventually she stopped. The boy dragged her further into the bushes, then ran away.

Isaac knew he'd witnessed a murder and that it was wrong to kill someone. But he didn't care about that. He saw murder stuff on the TV all the time, crime things were so boring. At this rate he'd be a hundred before he saw a girl without any clothes on. It was so unfair. He went downstairs and hoped a biscuit would cheer him up.

The Confession *(Gerald's Tale)*

Guilt is a terrible thing to live with. Gerald thought that if he went to prison, he'd feel it less. How naïve he was. Prison does many things to people, makes them feel a lot of things. Boredom, fear at the aggression of the other inmates, irritation at the constant noise, but not freedom from guilt. The police offered him a solicitor and he refused it. Part of him didn't want a fancy legal argument being pulled out of a hat. He needed to be punished. Which he thought was ironic as that's what had got him into that situation. He didn't do himself any favours at the police station. When they asked him for details he didn't give any, so they made up what they thought happened. The jury believed that version and so he got locked up. By the time he'd got over the shock of his life upending, it was too late. He could picture it all still, so clearly, as if it were days ago, rather than years.

If only his mobile hadn't been out of credit, and he hadn't been cut off on his home phone. The dispute over their charges had reached a stalemate and he'd refused to pay, which made them retaliate very heavy-handedly. If only he had sorted these things out, he'd never have gone to the phone box. Even though it was only at the end of his road, he had never had reason to use it before that day. The last phone box Gerald had used had been painted red with a heavy door that, when opened, had greeted him with a stale smell he recognised but didn't want to consciously identify.

The door had opened easily and as he stepped inside, he felt the draught around his feet, where the glass sides stopped a foot or so short of the ground. Although it was brightly lit, he didn't notice it at first or even while he stood talking. It wasn't until he was leaving that his eyes were drawn to the words.

Gerald hadn't needed to look up the number before he dialled, after all he had been ringing his sister every week for the past year. He'd done it ever since Mum had died, continuing the tradition she had started.

'Susan and you were so close as children, I don't want you drifting apart now you're grown up.' She had often said, 'you say a few words to her after I've told her all the things I want to.' And so she had dialled at precisely eight pm every Friday night and filled her daughter in on the weeks' happenings. Gerald had often been at a loss to find the few words his Mum wanted him to say. After all, the important events that had gone on in the preceding seven days, had already been told. That just left him with the minor incidents that happened to him at work, and sometimes even those his mum couldn't wait to tell Susan about and relayed the tale before he had his turn on the phone. As much as his mum wanted him and Susan to be close, the truth was that they never really had been, and so as they grew up they had inevitably drifted further apart. Mum had interpreted the peace that existed, when the two of them had been supposedly playing together, as reflecting a harmonious relationship. But it was more in fact that they were mutually disinterested and had merely ignored whatever it was that the other was doing.

Once Gerald had commented that it was unfair that they were always the ones to ring Susan and their mother had leapt to her defence, saying it wasn't much to do for her only daughter, just pay for a few phone calls. And she waited until it was after six, for it to be cheaper.

'After all, she hasn't got much money what with two children to support and that husband of hers only bringing in a pittance.' She had finished with an almost self-satisfied grin. Ever since Susan had first brought Mark home, Mum had prophesied that he was no good for her and she'd live to regret it. Susan should have settled down with Roger who worked in the building society and had good prospects, unlike Mark who was a self- employed plumber and was always in need of new customers. Susan had never lived to regret marrying Mark, as it turned out, and after Roger's stifling possessiveness, he was a welcome rescue. Try as she might, she could not convince Mum of this, and so had always listened in silence to the advice of what she should and should not have done. Mum's belief that a man's worth was entirely due to his ability to bring in good regular wages, could never be shaken.

It was in fact always a disappointment to her that Gerald was not more successful, and it was this that she entirely attributed his lack of success at securing himself a good wife. She never considered that he might first need to date a few girls before anyone would consider marrying him, or that it was odd that at the age of thirty-two he had never arranged to take a girl out for the second time. There had only been a scattering over the years that had ever agreed to go out with him at all, and for each of them, once had certainly been enough.

Gerald was not particularly worried that his social life was quiet. The girls he had in the past spent the evening with, had not been interested in listening to him talk about his life. He admitted he did talk about Mum rather a lot and would recite what he knew were her opinions on certain matters, but after all she was good to him, so deserved to play an important part in his life. Anyway, she was very wise. His other great love was God. Mum had brought them all up in strict accordance with the Catholic faith and Gerald had clung to its rules as a drowning man does to a life raft. Gerald thrived on being told what he was and wasn't allowed to do, and although now an adult, Mum continued to instruct him in correct behaviour, and he listened to every word she said, as well as to the Priest in the Sunday service. His attendance record at confession was impeccable. To do wrong was to be punished, that was his upbringing, either by man's laws, or more importantly by God's. The few girls he had been out with, had of course shared his passion for the Church. If only he had kept his interest in nice girls, none of the subsequent events would have happened. A life would have been saved.

It had been a surprise to Gerald, the amount of time his thoughts were occupied with images of Chrissie. She worked at the same factory that he did, working further down the line.

Gerald took custard cream biscuits off the conveyor belt that were misshapen or burnt. It was quite noisy in the factory, the machinery thundering constantly, even though mainly at the other end of the room, it echoed throughout the high-ceilinged building. Even so, the radio played all day, Radio One by popular demand, but not Gerald's choice. He preferred Radio Two, with its easy listening music and interesting discussions. When Gerald had put the suggestion forward to change the station, he was subjected to such ridicule and jokes from the others about him being old before his time, that he never brought the subject up again. For the most part, Gerald didn't let the remarks get to him, but it was the look Chrissie had given him that had been hurtful. He thought that was the first time he'd really noticed Chrissie.

She had only joined the company a few weeks before, one of a stream of young women that came for a regular wage and left soon after through lack of excitement. She dressed as most of them did, in short, tight skirts and low-cut T shirts pulled taut over her ample chest. She was certainly not the sort of girl that Mum would have approved of, as indeed Gerald himself didn't, in a fascinated kind of way.

After the suggestion over the radio, Gerald found himself thinking about her more and twice he'd been shouted at by Lee next to him on the line, for letting a lot of broken biscuits through. This upset him much more than anyone else would have been, as he prided himself on the quality of his work. He'd never had such a rebuke in the sixteen years he'd worked there. He forced himself to concentrate fully on his work. But by the next day, his resolve had broken and in the canteen he not only found himself standing near to her but trying to overhear her conversation with the girl next to her in the queue.

'How did you get on with Paul last night then?' the girl that Gerald knew was called Louise, asked.

'All right I suppose, he took me to the Indian at the end of the High Street.' Chrissie replied.

'And then what?'

'What do you mean and then what? I didn't let him do anything. Not for the price of a curry.'

'So is he taking you out again then, you know, try his luck next time?' Louise persisted.

'He can try all he likes, I don't fancy him all that much. He knocked the lager back like they were the last few bottles on earth.'

They shuffled slowly forward, but one of the canteen assistants had just left, so they knew it would be a while before they were served. Gerald was happy to stand there longer than usual, even though normally he would have grumbled at the remaining assistant when it finally got to his turn.

'They all drink too much. You can't be so choosy.' Louise replied.

'Oh can't I?' Chrissie said sharply, 'just because your Craig spends every night downing five pints at the Royal Oak, it don't mean that's what I want.'

'You leave my Craig out of this. You don't know him like I do, he's really sweet to me.'

'I'm sure he is.' Chrissie replied more soothingly, not wanting to create any unpleasantness with her friend, 'but I don't think Paul's the one for me anyway. He can take me to the cinema if he likes on Saturday though, I've been waiting to see that new Tom Cruise film for ages.'

As their coffees were passed over the counter to them, they moved out of earshot, and Gerald chose not to make himself conspicuous by following them down to the far end. As he sipped his own drink, he mulled over all of Chrissie's words. The poor girl obviously hadn't had much luck with boyfriends, what with having to eat in places such as Indian restaurants, something Gerald had never done, and putting up with excessive drinking. He himself was not one for having more than the odd sherry on special occasions and of course the sparkling wine at his sister's wedding. The idea began to emerge that he and Chrissie might be compatible.

As he sat on the bus that night travelling home, he felt an excitement he couldn't remember having known before. It was only tainted by the thought that he couldn't tell Mum all about it, but more the guilt that it was perhaps for the best that she would not be able to meet her, for they were bound not to have got along. The realisation that he was in effect pleased she was dead, made Gerald feel quite ill and he made a mental note to tell the priest about this in confession on Sunday. He needed to be admonished.

Over the following days, he watched Chrissie from what he hoped was a safe distance, admiring her and wondering how to make his feelings known to her. Part of the difficulty was he wasn't sure how he felt himself, he didn't know her well enough to think it could be love, and he wouldn't name his feelings as being of lust, although his body may have argued differently. He finally decided he would take things slowly and speak to her in a morning break.

It was two more days after he'd made this decision, that he was close enough to her, to ask the question.

'May I buy you a coffee?' he asked her directly, feeling hot all of a sudden.

'What?' Chrissie was taken aback.

'I just said, could I buy you coffee?' he replied.

'Oh, yeah okay, ta.' she said and stood next to him waiting for their turn at the counter. Gerald struggled to find some way of starting a conversation and in the end settled for, 'was it coffee you wanted, or would you prefer tea?'

'Coffee's fine ta.' she said.

'I know it's called a coffee break, but that's not what everyone drinks, is it?' he smiled at her.

The look she returned him could not be said to be a smile, with her brows knitted in bemusement. 'No, I suppose not.' she finally answered him.

Gerald was not encouraged by this start and was glad when, having handed the money over, he clutched their cups and led her towards an empty table. As soon as she sat down, Chrissie was looking about her, watching whoever came through the double doors.

'Were you waiting for someone?' Gerald asked at last.

'Only Louise. I always meet up with Louise.' she said, 'I expect she's in the lav.'

Gerald winced at this expression and hoped Louise would stay there for quite a while. It upset his plans somewhat, the knowledge that Louise would have to join them whenever she emerged. It meant he had to work faster, to get around to asking her to go out with him one evening. He decided he must start building up to it straight away.

'I think it's a shame there aren't more chances for people to talk to each other here. You know, we work together but don't get the chance to, well to talk. What do you think?'

'Never thought about it.' she replied, not taking her eyes off the doors, except to locate her cup and take a sip. 'You talk to who you want to, like me and Louise do.'

'And you and I are now.' he added eagerly. 'We've only got another ten minutes before we start again though.'

'Louise had better hurry, or she'll be gasping by dinner time.'

The mention of Louise's impending company spurred Gerald on.

'I was wondering if perhaps you'd like to go out somewhere one night?' he said at last.

'Go out?' There was a note of confusion in her voice.

'Yes, if you're free?' He fixed a smile on his face.

'What, like on a date, you and me?'

'Yes. I don't mind where you want to go. It doesn't have to be anywhere like that awful Indian place, and I don't drink beer.' he rushed the words out.

If she had just sat here and then said no, even brusquely, he thought afterwards it would have been all right. He could have coped, although somewhat unhappily with the thought that she didn't want to. He could have consoled himself that perhaps she didn't feel good enough for him. But instead, she had sat back and roared with laughter. There were even tears forming in the corners of each eye.

'You don't drink beer.' she managed to splutter in the midst of her laughing and rocked back and forth in her seat.

Gerald sat and watched, speechless. Others had turned to look at the source of all the noise, wondering what the joke was. He saw Louise come through the doors, and so did Chrissie, for she got up, grabbing her handbag from the back of the chair.

'I'm sorry Gerry,' she said at last, 'but I don't think so somehow.'

With that she walked over to Louise, still giggling as she went.

Not only had she hurt his pride, but she had called him the name he most loathed, Gerry. He had hated it at school when they had called him it and worse when it was written down spelt with a J. That was the name of that stupid cartoon mouse and sometimes awake at night, he could still remember the other boys circling around him, making squeaking noises and pouncing on him like a cat would, scratching and thumping him mercilessly. He had a perfectly good name of Gerald, named after his dear father. It was Gerald, not Gerry, not a hateful mouse, not a person to be bullied. And not to be laughed at.

The anger he felt about the incident welled in him until the whole episode had grown out of proportion. All day while he worked, he turned over various ideas of how to take revenge and the longer he thought, the more outrageous they became. It needed to be something that would disgrace and humiliate her, just as she'd done to him. Finally, he chose one, and decided he would see the supervisor in the afternoon break.

'May I have a word Mr. Mathews? Gerald asked, as he hovered outside the square glass enclosure serving as an office.

'If it's quick.' Dick Mathews sighed, sitting back down in his chair behind the desk.

Gerald stepped inside and shut the door behind him, but remained standing, thinking he shouldn't sit down since he had not been invited to.

'I'm afraid I must make a complaint.' Gerald said as assertively as he could manage.

'What about?' Dick asked, still leaning back in his seat, his hands clasped behind his head.

'Well it's about some money that's gone missing from my jacket pockets.' Gerald folded his arms, then let them drop by his sides, feeling uncomfortable.

'How much?'

Gerald was not prepared for this question. He struggled to come up with a figure. 'Ten pounds.' He finally said.

'Ten quid, is that all?'

'Well, about that, each time,' he improvised.

'What do you mean each time, how many times have there been?'

'About three or four.'

'And you haven't made a mistake, you know thought you had money in your jacket but put it in your trousers instead?'

'There's no mistake, it was definitely there each time.'

'Okay, leave it with me, I'll look into it.' Dick rose as he spoke and made to move toward the door.

'But that's not all' Gerald said.

'Oh, what then?'

'I know who did it.' Gerald's face was triumphant.

'How do you know? Are you sure?'

'Yes, very sure, I saw her myself the third and fourth times. I was watching you see, when everyone had gone to lunch. I stayed behind and hid.'

'Who was it then?'

'Chrissie Young.' Gerald delivered the name with a satisfied smile.

'Chrissie? You're not serious surely.' Dick said.

'I am very serious, I saw her take my money and I hope you're going to do something about it.' Gerald replied, his voice raised more than he knew it should be in front of his supervisor.

'All right, all right, keep your hair on. I'll talk to her and take the appropriate action.'

This time Dick moved over to the door and stood holding it open, waiting for Gerald to go through.

'Thank you.' Gerald managed and left feeling pleased he had put his plan into action.

Dick Mathews was left mystified by the encounter. Gerald wasn't one to lie he wouldn't have thought, but then equally he couldn't imagine Chrissie sneaking around during lunch breaks stealing money. Indeed if she had, why only from Gerald, which it must be, since no one else had complained. He would talk to her later.

Gerald watched from further down the factory, to see Dick Mathews beckon Chrissie in to see him. She went in without appearing distressed and sat down in the glass cubicle opposite him. At one point Gerald thought he heard her laughing, but knew that it must in fact have been crying and the sound simply distorted amidst the other noise of the room. He went on with his work, with a great sense of achievement.

Like Gerald, the factory owner was a deeply religious man and refused to be open for production on Sundays. Every other Monday was Gerald's day off in lieu of working every other Saturday, and so it was two days before he was back at work and able to find out what had happened to Chrissie. He was always amongst the first people to arrive for that shift and watched in disgust as others habitually arrived late at their posts, red faced and out of breath, using up the first five minutes of the company's time while they sorted themselves out. A situation that, in Gerald's opinion, something should be done about, with the offenders getting their pay docked at the very least.

By tea break Chrissie had still not turned up, and Gerald wondered if this was normally her day off. He tried to recall which days he had seen her last week, but could not be sure. All morning he kept thinking of reasons why she might not have come to work. Her mum might be ill, or she had gone to the dentist. Perhaps she'd had to go to a funeral even. But he knew deep inside what had really happened, why she was not there today and wouldn't be on any other day. He felt cold at the realisation of what he had done. He tried to console himself that he had only meant for her to get told off by Mr Mathews, to be made to feel like he had felt, small and humiliated. But Mr Mathews had taken his accusation seriously. There could only be one explanation, Chrissie had been sacked.

By lunchtime, his conscience was troubling him so much, he waited outside Mr. Mathew's office until his knock at the door was answered and he was invited inside.

'Gerald, what can I do for you?' Dick Mathews asked pleasantly.

'It's about Chrissie...'

'Well you've no need to worry.' he interrupted, 'I've spoken to her and it's all sorted. She's gone now and won't be coming back, so that should be the end of your troubles.'

'Gone?' Gerald managed to reply.

'Yes, you won't see her again.'

'It's just there may have been some, er, misunderstanding.' Gerald said.

'No, no need to worry, as I said I've spoken to her. Rest assured, I know what's what. All sorted out. Now it's time to get in that canteen queue I think, before all the best stuff goes eh?' He said standing up.

'Yes. Thank you' Gerald replied meekly and left.

As he sat looking at his usual salad roll, he knew he wouldn't be able to swallow any of it. The thought of eating after what he had done, made him feel quite sick. He left the roll where it was and went outside for some air.

Louise, in the absence of Chrissie, had sat next to Lee for a chat over her lasagne and chips.

'I wonder how Chrissie's getting on.' she said.

'I expect she's loving it.' Lee replied. 'She was right lucky there.'

'She always wanted to move over to the offices, said she was bored down in the factory. Funny the way it worked out isn't it. Fancy old Gerry coming up with that pack of lies about her stealing money from him. And all out of spite it was.'

'After he'd asked her on a date wasn't it?' Lee asked, and they laughed when Louise nodded in agreement.

'You're right, she was lucky to get that job though, mind you they were desperate for someone to go there quick.' Louise said, 'and what with her being friendly with Dick Mathews, I don't suppose she had any trouble getting transferred over.'

'I bet Gerry thinks he's got her the sack.' Lee said grinning and they laughed again.

'Serves him right if he does, silly sod.'

Louise looked at Lee as if for the first time, having not really taken much notice of him before, and wondered if he might be a candidate to replace her Craig. She gave him one of her alluring smiles in case she wanted to pursue him later.

Gerald thought the next few days were the most miserable he had ever spent. Several times he thought he should confess to Mr. Mathews and plead for her job back, but the fear of losing his own job was too overwhelming each time. More than anything else he wanted Mum. She would have understood why he had done what he had and probably said it was no more than that type of girl deserved. But she would have told him he had done wrong and convinced him to forgo some treat he would normally have enjoyed, in order to appreciate where his actions had led things. He could have rested more easily then, knowing she was right. Without her to confide in, he was at a loss. The closest person left, had to be his sister Susan. He contemplated ringing her for advice, but to speak to her at any time other than Friday nights was too alien an idea to consider. Instead he made himself wait those agonisingly long days until the week ended.

At five minutes to eight, he lifted the phone off its hook and dialled. To his dismay, there was no dial tone. He pressed the button several times to try and make a connection, but it was completely dead. Gerald sat there looking at it for minutes, realising that the phone company had finally carried out their threat and cut him off for not paying the bill. Despite his arguing the bill had to be wrong. He went and got his mobile out of his coat pocket and swore when he saw he'd let that run out of credit. He only knew how to top it up at the newsagents. He realised he could use the phone box at the end of the road. He grabbed his jacket and was still putting it on as he rushed down the road. He was thankful that he had plenty of change in his pocket and fed a fifty and a few ten pence pieces into the slot.

'Hello Susan, it's me Gerald.' He said as soon as she had picked up the phone. 'I expect you were starting to worry, since it's a few minutes past eight now.'

'Worry?' she said.

'Well never mind,' he replied, ignoring her lack of concern, 'how are you?'

'Fine, same as usual,' she began and proceeded to tell him about what the children had been doing all week.

Finally she asked, 'and what have you been up to then?'

This was his chance, here he could unburden himself onto her, just as he would have done to Mum. He stood there for a moment and was about to tell her the whole story, but when he tried to think how to start, he couldn't seem to find the right words. 'Nothing much.' was all he could manage.

'Well if you don't mind, Mark's calling me.'

'Yes, of course, I'll speak to you next week then, bye.' he replied.

'Bye.' She said.

Taking the change that had dropped down when he replaced the receiver, he opened the door. Glancing back to check he had left nothing behind, as Mum had always reminded him to do, he noticed it pinned up amongst others.

The small white card asked 'Do you want to be punished?' and had a drawing of a near-naked woman. Gerald stood there staring at it and he knew that this was the answer to his problem. He realised of course what sort of woman she was, what she did for a living, but it didn't stop him. At that moment he felt so desperate he didn't care. He dialled the number straight away.

'I've seen your card.' He began, as soon as a woman's voice had said hello.

'Oh yes?' She said.

'I want you to, well to do what you're offering.' He replied.

'It's fifty pounds.'

He thought for a moment but was interrupted.

'Cash of course.'

There was about that amount in the biscuit tin in the cupboard, saved for buying the weeks groceries. Her next words decided him.

'I'm free now if you wanted to come 'round.'

'Where are you?' He asked.

She gave him her address, which was only a few streets away and he agreed to go 'round after he had collected the money from home. By the time he reached her flat he was quite breathless, and uncomfortable in his thick woollen jumper. She opened the door on his first knock and stood there unashamedly in a skirt that ended just below her hips.

'I rang,' he began, 'my name's Gerald.'

'That's nice for you.' She said and led the way into the bedroom. 'You got the money?'

'Yes.' He handed her the bundle of notes he had carefully counted out at home and watched while she flicked through them before putting away in a drawer. Up close she was younger than he had thought she would be and he felt a little disappointed. He had wanted her to be a lot older than him, as his mum would have been.

'Take that off.' She said sharply, nodding at his jumper.

'Good idea, I am rather hot.' He replied, not seeming to notice her tone.

'Now your trousers. Come on chop, chop,' She clapped her hands together as she said the last words.

'No, I don't want to do that.' He said shaking his head.

'Hmm, I'll allow that for now. But I may have to be sterner with you.'

She walked over to her wardrobe and opened the door. Hanging on the back was an array of leather belts and curled up, a long, black bullwhip. Set across these on two hooks, were a cane and a riding crop.

'Which of these do you deserve then?' She asked as she ran her hand over the riding crop and cane.

'No, not them.' Gerald said, horrified.

'Well then, maybe these.' She let the belts fall through her fingers as she ran her hand backwards and forwards as if they were strings on a harp.

She took one down and curled one end of it around her hand.

'I think you've been a naughty boy, haven't you?' She stepped towards him, slapping the belt gently against her leg.

'Yes.' was all he could manage as he stood there unable to move.

'And so you need to be punished, don't you?' She asked.

'Yes,' he said, then knowing how wrong this whole situation was added, 'No, I don't.'

'I think you do. And the more disobedient you are to me, the harsher I'm going to have to be with you.' She stepped nearer.

'No.' he shouted.

'That's enough Gerry.' She moved her hand upwards and the belt sailed close to him.

At that moment he snapped. She had done just what Chrissie had, called him Gerry and was standing in front of him, grotesque, offering to beat him. He pushed her back, hard, harder than he meant to and watched as she fell. Her left foot twisted in its high stiletto shoe and she went backwards, hands flying upwards grasping the air, trying to find something to hold onto. He winced as he heard the crack when her head hit the brass bedstead and stared as she lay motionless on the floor. A trickle of blood ran out from under her blonde hair and soaked into the carpet. The dark red stain slowly grew bigger.

Gerald stood there with a feeling of panic rising in him. He reached his hand towards her neck and hovered a few inches away but couldn't make himself actually touch her. He held his hand close to her mouth, but he couldn't feel any breath. She wasn't moving, her chest wasn't rising and falling as it should have been. It was just the blood stain that was moving, getting bigger.

He sprang to his feet, grabbed his jumper from the floor and rushed out of the front door. He ran down the street he had walked along not more than fifteen minutes before. Other pedestrians had given him strange looks as he had barged past them, his jumper trailing behind him. It had caught around one schoolgirl's arm, giving her the opportunity to hurl abuse at him, but none of these happenings made him slow down.

When he had finally let himself into the flat and closed the door behind him, he leant against it gasping for air. Eventually he could breathe normally again, and he slid down to the floor exhausted. Gerald sat there whilst outside it grew dark. He dared not venture further inside but could not have said why he was frightened to even sit down in an armchair, rather than be on the cold, uncarpeted floor in the hallway. It was almost as if he felt his body weight against the door could keep out those that were going to come after him for the crime he had just committed.

His throat was dry from the unaccustomed running and when he could stand it no longer, he gingerly got up. His legs were stiff, and he could only take small steps at first, but it was worth it when he had made it into the kitchen and greedily drunk two glasses of water. Now he had moved away from the front door, he felt braver and tried to decide what he should do next. He knew he should go down to the police station and turn himself in, but since Mum was not there to tell him to, he could not make himself go. As he thought of Mum, the answer came to him as to what he should do, to go where he should have gone in the first place, to confession. Before he could change his mind, he left the flat and walked straight to the Church of the Sacred Heart.

It was almost dark within the church, and as soon as he stepped inside, he felt calmer. There was no priest there, so he sat on a pew by the confessional, knowing whatever he said in there was in total confidence. The priest could give him absolution if he was truly sorry, as he was, and he would make this awful feeling of guilt, go away. As the minutes ticked by, the urge to get his confession over and done with became stronger. Every time the heavy wooden door opened he looked around, hoping the moment had arrived.

An elderly woman sat down on the end of his pew. From the side, she looked a little like Mum, with her straight grey hair. Gerald edged himself nearer and said, 'hello.'

'Hello.' She replied and turned towards him inquiringly.

'I'm waiting for a priest.' He said.

'Me too.' She answered.

'I must give him my confession you see. I've done something terribly wrong, well more than one thing really.' Before he realised what he was doing, he was telling her the whole sordid tale. He tried to explain what he had felt for Chrissie, how humiliated he had been when she had turned him down and his need for retribution. The guilt he felt afterwards when she'd been dismissed had driven him, he said, to go to that woman and led him to do such a dreadful thing as to kill her.

All the while, the woman sat listening to him, not saying anything, but her expression changing from polite interest to one of disgust. When he had finished and was sitting there saying over and over he hadn't meant to, she got up and left the church.

Gerald didn't even notice, he had buried his face in his hands, saying he was sorry. He rocked back and forth and sobbed.

He was interrupted from his private misery by a hand tapping on his shoulder.

'I believe you need to talk to us sir.' A man in a police uniform said.

Unwanted Intruder *(Roberta's Tale)*

Roberta heard the phone ring just as she was turning the key in the door. She hated it going to answerphone and the nuisance of calling back. It was likely to be her grandmother as she was one of the few people who rang the landline. Granny was getting really frail now, so to not speak to her when she'd called, could mean she missed her needing some urgent help. She counted the rings, it got to four and she knew on the sixth one it would stop and the recording would start.

She struggled with the weight of her shopping bags so dropped one in the hall and carried the lighter one into the kitchen with her. She picked up the phone from where it was plugged in on the worktop.

'Hello.' She said.

'Good afternoon madam, I'm calling from Microsoft.' The man said.

'Are you?' she replied, knowing instantly it was a scammer. 'Oh dear, what's the problem?'

'We have detected some error messages from your IP address and I'm sorry to tell you, this means your account has been hacked.' He didn't sound particularly sorry.

'That's terrible, what does it mean?' She replied, her primary school nativity actor reappearing.

'Your data is at risk of being stolen and your files corrupted.'

'So I'll lose everything!' She was getting into character nicely now, even if she hadn't done terribly well as the innkeeper's wife, reiterating there was no room.

'We might be able to help you keep hold of the essentials.'

'Thank goodness you rang and told me. Do I need to turn the computer on?'

'Yes please.'

'I'll do that. I'll pop the phone down and get it started. It's quite slow. You won't go away will you, even if it takes a while?' She put some panic in her voice.

'No madam, I will stay right here.'

As quietly as she could, she took some of the shopping out of the bag and put the cold items in her fridge. The tins she put away as quietly as she could. She picked up the phone and told him it was still starting up and he said that was fine.

She went into the hall to pick up the other bag and was upset to see that she hadn't shut the front door. Ever since the break-up, she'd hated living alone, even though she'd been fine all the years before Bradley had been with her. She'd really enjoyed the sense of protection she felt when he was around, even if it was just to catch a spider for her or worse, a daddy long-legs that had managed to fly in. She just hoped that nothing had come in whilst she'd been in the kitchen. She picked up the handset again. 'It's doing updates, so I don't know how to get into anything. Is this part of what's wrong, is that why it's doing this?' She said, sounding distressed. 'I do all my banking online, how am I going to get back into that?' She smiled to herself for the hook she was giving him.

'Yes it could be part of the problem, but don't worry, we have experts here who can help restore it.'

'I can't thank you enough. I've just got to pop to the loo, I'm afraid I'm rather desperate. Can you wait still? I really need your help.'

'Of course madam, you go ahead.'

She finished putting the rest of the shopping away and wished she could have put the kettle on for a nice cup of tea. She was still a bit chilled from being outside. She knew it wouldn't be long before the scammer hung up on her, so she decided to switch it on anyway.

'I'm back. I've put the kettle on as it sounds as if we're going to be at this a while.' She said cheerily.

'Is it ready now? What can you see on your desktop?'

'The desk is really messy. Hold on. I'll see if I can find some paper. I'm going to need to write all this down.'

Having said she needed to go to the toilet, she realised now that she actually did. She decided she'd played along for enough time. 'So, we've been on the phone now for ten minutes and 14 seconds.' She said.

'Yes madam, is your computer on now?'

'No, because I haven't switched it on, because I know you're not from Microsoft, but I have managed to waste ten minutes of your time, which is ten minutes you couldn't scam someone else. Goodbye.' She heard him swear as she hung up. She put the phone down with a grin.

She went to the bathroom upstairs, as she planned to change into her pyjamas straight after. Her dressing gown was lovely and soft, and she'd enjoy snuggling up in it with a cup of tea. She pushed the door behind her even though Bradley wasn't living there anymore to embarrass her, but she no longer bothered to close it completely. When she was washing her hands, she looked at herself in the mirror and thought she looked a bit tired. She would definitely have an early night.

Her heart suddenly started racing as she felt a sense of dread, seeing the door open. She made herself turn around and face who the intruder was. At first she couldn't see anyone. Then she saw him.

He decided to speak first. 'Meow,' as he walked over to her and rubbed his long black fur against her leg.

She laughed with relief. 'Hello, who are you then eh?' She bent down to see if he had a collar. He didn't so she decided she'd have to take him outside and hope he made his way home. 'You gave me such a fright.'

He purred as she stroked the top of his head and under his chin.

'Come on you.' She walked out of the bathroom and he followed her as she'd hoped.

She didn't yet know that a teenage boy was downstairs, rifling through her handbag.

Forgiving Nature *(Harley's Tale)*

I try to tell myself that Gran would have forgiven me, but of course I can never know for sure. She did have a forgiving nature, I do know that. I think about the time she gave me permission to have a few friends 'round, while she was away visiting her best friend. Forty could be called a few, couldn't it? I'd tried to argue that I thought she'd realise that word would get 'round via social media and there'd be more than a dozen or so she'd have had at a party of her own. And when the shock of what they'd done to the walls had worn off, she said as long as I put it right, we'd say no more about it. I couldn't fathom what they'd been thinking of or probably more likely, what they'd taken to make them do such a thing. It also hadn't occurred to me that I should have locked away the paint and brush that I'd been using to touch up the back door. Why didn't I know what was going on at the time? My answer to that was clear from how hungover I felt the next day.

Gran had asked what exactly it was that they'd drawn. I couldn't tell her the truth. Eventually I suggested it might be a landscape, maybe with two hills and a mountain in the middle, but I said it didn't matter, I'd paint over it right away. I suggested she go back to her friend's whilst I sorted it. I asked if she'd like the whole room done in a new colour and she liked that idea, so I went and bought paint in her favourite duck egg blue. When she got back, she said she liked it and true to her word, it wasn't mentioned again. I didn't push my luck to ask for any more parties though. Gran was lovely but she wasn't stupid.

She was much more of a mum to me than Jo, my real one. Mum was always too busy for me, getting to know her latest boyfriend. This one could be 'the one' she'd say. She was the eternal optimist as none of them ever lasted more than a few months, what with her moods and histrionics. As for Dad, I couldn't even remember what he looked like. So, although I officially lived in Avon Street with Mum, so that she could get all the child benefit and whatever, I actually spent my waking hours in Durham Close. There I got the love and attention I craved.

Gran didn't have a go at me when I got things wrong, she just said we'd learn from it and move on. No point in dwelling on the past she'd say. I knew she was thinking about Jo and how she'd blamed herself somehow for how she was. I wondered if Jo might be bipolar, but whenever I suggested to her that she should go to see her GP, she'd turn on me, saying they only wanted to lock up people like her. People who liked a bit of fun, but who let life get on top of them sometimes. She went as far as saying that, if I said anything else about pills and just having a chat with someone, she wouldn't have anything more to do with me. Although she wasn't a great mum, she was still mine and so like a coward, I backed off.

I don't know if I'd go so far as to say I loved Jo, but I knew for sure that I did love Gran. And for good reason. I owed her everything, including inspiring me to work hard at school, so that I got some pretty good exam results. Good enough for me to go to uni. I didn't really want to stay away, as I was worried how she'd cope. But it was obvious that Exeter had exactly the right course for me, and she wouldn't hear of me going somewhere that was second choice. So I went and came home the odd weekend, and always when term ended. At first it was all worked out and Gran was all right on her own. But then she had the stroke. She was found by the postman, who'd seen her lying face down in the hallway. She'd been there for hours by all accounts and she was really poorly when they took her into hospital. I came back on the first coach as soon as I heard, and it was the longest journey ever.

When I got to her bedside, I hardly recognised her. She seemed to have aged ten years, even though it hadn't even been three weeks since I'd last seen her. She seemed smaller and she'd lost some use of her right arm as well as not being able to talk very well. She drifted in and out of sleep that first visit and I cried when I got back to the house, great noisy sobs as if my whole world had come to an end. I rang Jo, but she said she wouldn't be able to visit for a day or so, as she said Pietro's family were visiting from Florence and she didn't have long to get to know them. And she said Gran wasn't actually dying was she? When I said no, she just said, well then, she'd pop over in a couple of days' time.

I couldn't remember ever feeling so alone. I rang some of my uni mates, but they didn't understand. I needed a girlfriend, one who knew what it meant to really care about someone. But I'd split up with my latest one a few weeks before. I decided the best remedy was to meet up with some of my old school friends and get completely pissed.

I stayed away from uni for about three weeks in total, doing a bit of studying, but even though I watched the recordings of the lectures, I found it hard to concentrate. Gran was slowly recovering and she could speak fairly well now, but she hadn't regained much use of her arm. The occupational therapist had been round to talk to her about whether or not she could cope back at her house and social services were doing a report. Gran was adamant, she was going to return there and she wouldn't go into a home. They'd said maybe she should consider it more seriously as the doctors were saying she was at risk of another stroke. She eventually agreed to carers coming in twice a day and wearing a pendant round her neck, where she could press the button to summon help if needed. And so it worked out all right at first. She persuaded me she was doing fine and packed me back off to uni.

It was the second stroke that really hit her. She was back in hospital but longer this time. Jo did make a quick visit, but then couldn't be found for days afterwards. So the question of Gran going home arose. Again she said she wouldn't go into a care home, even though I begged her to because I was so worried about her all on her own. What if she fell down the stairs I kept asking. I really couldn't bear the thought of what might happen to her. I pressed her on what she had against the idea. I pointed out she didn't go out and about anymore. Most of her days were spent dozing in front of the television and she could do that anywhere. Her friends could visit her just as easily in the home as at her house.

She said something quite surprising then, about Grandad and how he was the love of her life. I'd always known that, she always talked about him as if he'd be home any minute and there were photos all 'round the house. Her two great sorrows in life were losing her husband when he was only fifty-two and Jo being so "unsettled".

'This was our home, me and your Grandad's. When I leave it permanently, it'll be in a coffin.'

'You didn't live here at the beginning though, did you?' I asked her.

'No. We had a nice three-bed semi up by the common. Lovely it was, views all across the hills and close to the shops.'

'Why did you move to Durham Close then?' I asked, vaguely remembering there being a specific reason why they'd relocated.

'It didn't feel the same after we were burgled. Never felt safe after that.' And she'd gone on to talk about Grandad doing the decorating and how he'd dropped a wet paintbrush on the dog and what a palaver that was to wash it off.

She wasn't to know I thought I'd found the answer. For her own sake, I'd have to make it unappealing to go back to the house. Then the care home would become an attractive option.

So I got in touch with my old school friends, Luke and Ryan. They'd spent their lives in and out of trouble, including Luke having a short spell in prison. They knew exactly how to break into a property. I told them not to do anything too drastic. Knock a few chairs over, open a few drawers, that sort of thing. They wanted to know what they could keep for their troubles and so I said the TV was quite new. Otherwise, everything was not worth anything second-hand, but they weren't to touch her jewellery. That couldn't be replaced and I didn't want her without her special things. What they were welcome to, was the £500 in notes that Gran had in a sock in the airing cupboard. I'd told Gran a hundred times that wasn't a safe place to keep money, but she said she liked to have it for emergencies. Well her failing health felt like an emergency to me. She was due home from hospital and it wasn't safe for her to be living alone. I'd even offered to come home and redo the year at uni, but she was furious at the suggestion and so no more would be said about that.

I kept telling myself I couldn't have known. She was supposed to be in hospital for another week, before the next decision was made. I was going to visit the house and take photos of the mess the burglars had made and show her in her hospital bed. Then she'd have said she didn't want to go back there after all and happily agree to going into the home.

I couldn't have predicted she'd have a row with the nurses and call herself a taxi. She shouldn't have been allowed to leave, she wasn't strong enough, but with the pressure on staff and finding beds, I suppose they were happy to let her go.

It was the flashing blue lights and a police officer that greeted me and stopped me from rushing into the house, when I arrived ready to be 'surprised' by the burglary. I couldn't work out how they knew. The officer was very kind. She sat me down on the step and explained Gran had let herself into the house and that was where she'd died. They wouldn't let me in, but I could see through the open door that Luke and Ryan had done a thorough job messing up the place. Certainly thorough enough for Gran to feel scared out of her wits, bringing on her third and final stroke.

I saw her in that special room they have in the hospital, where the dead can be laid out for viewing. I didn't want to look at her at first. I felt so guilty, so ashamed that I'd killed her. Would she have forgiven me when she knew I'd only done it with the best of intentions? I had to believe she would. In the end it was Jo, of all people, that allowed me to sleep easy at night. Never one to sugar-coat anything, one day she said, 'it's lucky really, Mum dying like that.'

'How do you make that out?' I asked.

'She'd have hated it in a home and she wouldn't have been safe here. So dropping dead in your own house, nice and quick, that's not a bad end. I reckon she wouldn't have minded.'

'Really?' I so wanted that to be true.

'But makes you think, doesn't it.' She said.

'About what?' I asked.

'You've got to make the best of your life, 'cos you've only got the one and you never know when your number's up.'

I nodded.

'I was thinking maybe I should go down the doctors. Mum wanted me to. Been on at me for years.'

'Worth a try.' I said, trying not to be pushy.

'You come with me?' she asked.

'Course I will.' I hesitated. It had been such a long time since I'd said it. 'Course I will Mum.'

I started to feel my load lighten, just a tiny bit, until she said, 'the police reckon they know who burgled the house.'

'Do they?' I was in a panic but desperate not to show it. The police were never supposed to have known about the so-called burglary. I would have persuaded Gran not to bother reporting it as it would be more stress. I'd sort the house out put it all back how it should be.

'Yes, got some fingerprints and they're just tracking them down.' Mum said. 'At least the guilty will be brought to justice.'

I wondered if that would include me.

Retire for Life *(Hugh's Tale)*

Hugh felt the familiar fear when someone knocked on his door unexpectedly. Despite the number of years that had passed since it happened, he never stopped worrying that someone would put the pieces together and he'd be arrested. He supposed he'd never know complete peace of mind.

He left it for a couple of minutes, hoping that whoever was at his door would go away, but he heard the knocking again, more insistent. He got up and took a deep breath. He shuffled along the next few steps in case he was being watched through the glass in the front door. He hung his head to one side and as he opened the door, he adopted a look that his late wife would have described as pathetic. He was an old man now and he felt pathetic, he had been for so many years, perhaps all his adult life. But these days he needed others to see him like that, so he exaggerated his failing health to make sure they took pity on him or at least saw him as harmless.

'Hello,' he mumbled, 'what can I do for you?'

'Mr Baxter is it?' the young woman with an iPad asked. She smiled at him.

'Yes.' Hugh replied, nervous as to who was looking for him.

'I'm Amy Fitzpatrick, Social Services. Your GP made a referral. Can I come in?' She showed him the ID badge hanging from the lanyard around her neck. She lifted her foot up and was poised to enter the house.

'I don't need anything thanks.' Hugh said and gently tried to push the door.

Obviously used to this kind of greeting, Amy took a step closer to the threshold, held her hand out to stop the door and smiled straight at him. 'No problem. If I can just get your signature to say that, I can leave you in peace. Just a couple of papers to sign.'

She leant forward and Hugh automatically stepped back, opening the door wider. He believed her line of only needing a signature and it wasn't until he was sitting at his kitchen table opposite her that he realised he'd revealed all the troubles he was genuinely experiencing now as well as the extra details he'd added for so many years.

He was frail now and his GP was right to be worried, but he tried to stay off anyone official's radar if he possibly could. And whilst he'd managed to do that for the last thirty years, he wondered how he would keep it up when he got much older. And what if he had dementia and started saying things about his past? He had to hope people wouldn't believe him and think they were the ramblings of a disturbed mind. Well he had been disturbed, he must have been to do what he did. He had to force himself to concentrate on what he was being asked by this woman.

'And you say the driver tried to blame you?' Amy looked upset on his behalf.

'That's right. He said I stumbled into the road and there was no way anyone could have stopped in time. I was hurt pretty badly. I can't remember a thing before the accident, and I was in such a mess I think they cut my clothes off me and threw them away with my wallet inside them. Months I was in that hospital. They said even my own mother wouldn't have recognised me, I was so badly injured.'

'Do they do dental checks for ID, like they do when you've been murdered, to find out who you really were?' Amy asked, clearly interested to know.

'If they did, it didn't come up with any answers.'

'Social Services must have looked after you then, if you weren't very strong when you left hospital and you were all alone in the world. And you got to choose yourself a new name. Why did you choose Hugh?'

'It was on the doctor's name badge.' He said, remembering seeing the word when he came 'round. He'd known straight away that was his own name, but not much else, except a strong sense something was very wrong. It was as if the information was just out of reach, the same as when he tried to remember someone else's name. He knew it was in him, but couldn't bring it to mind.

It was only a few hours later that memories started to come back. Given the horrifying detail, he knew he had to keep up the pretence of a lost memory. He knew all too well what happened in his house on that last day and all those months leading up to it, when he wasn't himself. That's how he consoled himself, that it was so out of character. Or when that excuse didn't ring true, he tried to believe it was his manager's fault, for setting it all in motion.

At the age of 55 his branch manager had, more insisted than offered, him the chance to take early retirement. His career at All For The Office had been static for more than eight years and he had not reached even his first goal of rising to sales manager. He had remained as one of their salesmen all the time he had been with them, each year he had only just met his targets for getting new business. It could not be said that he didn't work hard, for he had thrown himself into the job from the day he had joined. If ever a representative from the branch was needed for going on a conference, he always offered himself as a volunteer, eager to hear about new products joining the range of stationery they sold. He was often the first one to arrive in the office each day, and could be seen returning after a long day travelling through the congested streets of outer London to see his prospective customers, to finalise his paperwork. Unfortunately, this dedication was not fully appreciated by his superiors, since, as they told him at his six-monthly performance reviews, he was there solely to bring in new orders. It was the amount of money he brought into the company and nothing else. They wouldn't have minded if he spent half his week playing golf, if the rest of the time he brought in more business than he was doing.

In an effort to help him along, they had sent him on courses to brush up his sales skills. As usual, he had looked forward to them and was a dedicated student. The reports back to his branch had noted this and also confirmed that he had demonstrated to them perfectly well how to follow the sales process and overcome objections. The tutors could only suggest that perhaps when he was out on the road he was more aggressive than he had been in their role play exercises. Maybe he should remember to be friendly, in a business-like manner, whilst gently manoeuvring the prospective customer towards a sale. They could offer no further explanation for why he was not more successful. Hugh could not say why either, since he had followed every bit of advice that he was given, to the letter. He often said it was almost as if someone just got there ahead of him, who knew what price he was going to quote, and offered the same service for less. The final straw had been when he lost what would have been the company's largest order.

It had been one of Hugh's most exciting days, when he had come back into the office from visiting the purchasing manager, Mr. Johnson of the multi-million pound A.M.C.T. Corporation. He had been trying for weeks to get this second appointment with them after he had already had an initial visit and they'd discussed their existing purchases and an approximate figure of how much they were willing to spend. Since then, he had put countless hours into his preparation, and many nights sitting up working.

Occasionally it crossed his mind how bored his wife Catherine must be, hearing about it so often. He was now a familiar figure at the library from doing so much research on them, always trying to anticipate what else their organisation might need, what added value his company might be to them. The business directories he had looked through had been useful in supplying information on how they operated and how many employees they had. He had delivered his presentation as perfectly as he could have wished to, without any sign of nervousness. His sales manager had accompanied him and had also been impressed with the way he delivered it, particularly noticing how interested A.M.C.T. seemed to become, the more Hugh talked.

It was to both their surprise when the letter came from them, politely thanking them for their time but firmly stating that their services would not this time be required. Hugh had telephoned. Mr Johnson immediately, but been told curtly that his letter was self-explanatory, they had just put an order in elsewhere, but perhaps he would like to get in touch with them to try again next year. Hugh went home early that day, unable to put on a brave face to cover up his disappointment.

When Hugh went into work the next day, he was called into the branch manager's office.

'Hugh, sit down won't you.' Eric Barrington said.

'Thanks.' Hugh sat down, unsure of what was going to be said to him.

'I would like to offer you an opportunity Hugh. A new start.'

'Really?' Hugh was pleasantly surprised.

'Yes. I've been contacted by Head Office and they rather feel that we are over-staffed.' Eric said.

Hugh looked at him blankly, unable to connect this to the opportunity of a new start.

'I'm pleased to be able to give you the chance to take early retirement.'

'Retirement?' Hugh stared at him incredulously.

'That's right.' Eric continued. 'It will mean a generous lump sum and a more than adequate pension that can start straight away.'

'But I'm only 55.' Hugh said. 'I can't retire now.'

'That's what I mean about a new start. Look at it as a means to begin something different. Take up a new kind of career if you like, with the security of that lump sum and pension to back you up.' Eric folded his arms, congratulating himself that he was making it sound an attractive proposition. Getting into his stride he added, 'But before you do that, you could take a long holiday, spend a bit of time with that lovely wife of yours. What's her name again?'

'Catherine.'

'Catherine, of course it is. Look why not talk it over with her tonight and you can give me your decision in the morning.'

'Really Eric there's no need to talk to her about it. I have no intention of retiring now. I like my job, I'm good at it.'

'But are you Hugh?' Eric asked in a kind tone, such as he'd use to a young child.

Hugh couldn't think how to reply. He had always worked so hard, often at the expense of how little time he spent at home, he deserved better results than he had got. It was true that he had never excelled.

'Think it over carefully, before you give me a rash answer. After all, where did you envisage your career with us would go?'

'Up to sales manager, I had always hoped.' Hugh answered.

'To be frank Hugh, there is simply no chance of that happening. You can see the way the company is going, it's promoting younger people these days, not those, well, more mature.'

'I see.'

'I doubt I'll ever get further up the ladder than this.' Eric added in an attempt to empathise.

They looked at each other and both knew this was not true, Eric was still only in his mid- thirties and had the "killer instinct" that Head Office demanded from its senior staff. Eric handed him a set of papers.

'Look these are the details of the offer. Go home now and read them if you like.'

Hugh took the outstretched paperwork automatically and stood up.

'You'd do well to accept Hugh.' Eric said without smiling and left the room.

Going home early two days in a row was not appealing to Hugh. Catherine had not been there and wouldn't be today either, and the house had seemed so quiet. He sat down at his desk and leafed through the papers he had just been given. The sum on offer and annual income were much higher than he would have guessed at. The suddenness of it all was too overwhelming to allow him to rationally see that he would be getting a good deal. He looked around the room at the three other salesmen that were in, but none of them met his eye. Hugh realised they all knew. After sitting there for over an hour, he could take the unusual silence no longer and went down to the pub. After downing some whiskies, he finally gave in and went home.

Catherine was surprised to see Hugh home before her, for the second time that week.

'Everything all right?' She asked as she planted the customary kiss on his cheek.

'No, it is not.' He growled at her. He was more than a little drunk by now.

'What's up?' she asked.

'They're putting me out to pasture, on the scrap heap.' he slurred at her.

'Redundancy?'

'No, early retirement.' He almost spat the words at her.

'Surely not at your age.' She said in disbelief.

'That's what I said, but it seems my get up and go has got up and gone.' He reached for the whisky bottle and found himself a glass.

'I think you've had enough of that darling.' She tried to take the bottle out of his hand.

He pushed her back roughly and she almost lost her balance. 'No I haven't. You leave me alone.'

She stood there swaying a little before him, adding to the room that was already spinning slightly to his drunken eyes. He narrowed them and looked at her properly for the first time since she had come home. She looked smart in her crimson suit and crisp white blouse.

'What you all dolled up for, where have you been?'

'To work of course, where else? Look I'm going to get changed. I'll put the kettle on and make you some coffee when I come down.' She left him, knowing it would only rile him further if she tried to talk sensibly to him, while he was in this state. He'd never taken any interest in her own work, and she knew he wasn't in a good state of mind to reassure him they would be fine for income, from his retirement and her wages. He'd need to be a lot calmer to hear that.

When she returned with the coffee, she looked more familiar to him in her jumper and flower print cotton skirt. She turned the television on as a distraction and sat down in the armchair furthest away from him. After he had dozed off, she tipped the rest of the whisky down the sink and replaced the bottle back next to him, hoping he would think he had drunk it all. When he woke up, it had seemed to have worked, he picked up the empty bottle and held it to the light.

'I must have been well out of my tree, I don't remember knocking back that much?' he said. 'My head's splitting. How long have I been asleep?'

'Almost four hours. It will nearly be time to go to bed, but I don't know if you'll sleep again so soon. Do you want some tablets for your headache?'

'Yes please, and some more of that coffee you make so well love.'

She got what he had asked for and automatically made him a sandwich.

'Thought you might be hungry by now.' She said as she handed it to him.

'Now you come to say that, I am, ta.'

He took it from her and wolfed it down.

'I've read the offer they made to you, it seems very generous.' She said.

'I suppose.' he replied with a mouthful of the tomato she had carefully sliced up and added to the cheese.

'Taking the package is one thing. But you don't want to actually retire now do you?' A worried look came over her face.

'No I don't. But it seems I don't really have any choice to leave.'

'I see.'

'So I'm going to take the money and just get another job. We'll be quids in. Besides I'll be able to spend more time with you. You'd like that wouldn't you?'

'Yes of course, but really I'm not here very often.'

'Why not?'

'I work too.' She'd long ago stopped resenting his disinterest and used it to her advantage to do what work she enjoyed.

'Oh that little job of yours, well you don't have to go in if you don't want to. After all it's only a bit of typing and that isn't it?'

'It's more than that, but the main thing is I like working Hugh.'

'You could drop back to being part-time again. You said it was only going to be for a while anyway, 'till your boss got someone to do it permanently. You know I never liked you going out to work in the first place.'

'Well I'll see whether or not I can do a few less hours,' she soothed. 'I think I'll go up to bed now, why don't you try and get some proper sleep as well?'

'I'll be up in a minute.' he said as he sat back in his chair, but before she had reached the top of the stairs, he had nodded off again.

Catherine decided to leave him asleep downstairs. The thought of him snoring next to her and breathing alcohol in her face, was not appealing.

Hugh went into the office the next day, aching all over and with a hangover, but he refused to let it show. Knowing he had no choice, he accepted the early retirement package with good grace. The news quickly spread around his colleagues, and they were soon coming up to him saying how lucky he was to have escaped. The customary comments were made about how he would now have time to play golf whenever he wanted to. Hugh did not enlighten them to the fact that he couldn't play and had no interest in it, but merely agreed with everyone. He told them of plans he had got to go on some exotic holidays with Catherine, and then get another job somewhere in his own good time, certainly not before the summer was over. He said he would enjoy lazing in his garden, rather than sitting in his car in traffic jams. He'd be thinking of them he added, as he lounged with some good books and cool drinks while they drove around in the heat. Talking in this vein he almost convinced himself that it was for the best.

That Friday was his last day, after hardly having had time to finalise everything he had started. He had been encouraged to pass on work from the moment he had accepted their offer and soon started to feel unwanted. After a few drinks in the pub at lunchtime, Eric assembled everyone together and made a brief speech. He told of Hugh's contribution to the success of the company, how he would be greatly missed, but that it was Catherine's gain to have him around more. The session was rounded off with a presentation. A collection had been taken and card signed by the whole branch. As Hugh stood there listening to Eric, he felt sad that he would no longer be part of the team, realising that they would all come in again on Monday whereas he would be left at home. He waited in anticipation to find out what their gift would be. An oblong box was handed to him, wrapped in shiny paper. He opened it up, not wanting to wait to see how much they thought of him and saw that it was a brass carriage clock. Forcing a smile, he thanked them all and they gave him a round of applause.

Going back to his desk for the last time, he set the clock down, unable to believe how unimaginative they had been. His disappointment was immense. Packing his few personal items in his briefcase, as well as the clock and card, he waved goodbye to them all and left. It was still only three o'clock.

Catherine found him in a sullen mood that evening when she returned and tried to show enthusiasm for the present they had given him, finding room for it on the mantelpiece.

'Isn't it heavy. It looks very expensive.' She lied to him, thinking it was probably made in China. 'It goes well up there.'

'Do you think so?' Hugh was cheered up by that thought.

They went away that weekend, knowing Hugh would feel miserable if they just spent the time at home. Most of the time he was quite buoyant and talked about all the different careers he might now embark upon.

'Have you spoken to your boss about working less hours?' Hugh asked as they sat waiting for their main course to be served in the restaurant.

'Yes, but he said it wasn't that convenient at the moment, perhaps soon though.'

'Well can't you tell him it's not convenient to me to have you working so much? This is our chance to spend some time together. After all, I'll be starting a new job soon no doubt and then the opportunity will have passed.' He took a sip of the wine and waited for her to agree.

'We're just so busy at the moment. I'm sure it will settle down any time now. Is the wine all right for you, not too sweet?'

'Not bad. Surely they can spare you though, I mean you're only a secretary. Besides, I'll need you at home more, there will be more to do around the house since I'll be there all day, for the time being anyway.'

'There's no need to worry about the housework, I've asked Bridget to come in twice a week.' Catherine told him.

'Bridget? Ah that woman you mentioned who helps with the spring cleaning.' He gulped down the wine, relieved that at least he wasn't going to be left in the house to do the dusting. He thought perhaps it would all work out all right.

The first few weeks went much more quickly than Hugh had even dared hope they would. He found it took quite a while to fill out job application forms and attend interviews. More than once he said it was a full time occupation, looking for a job. When the weather was warm, he even managed to do what he had joked about to his ex-colleagues and sat reading in the garden with a cold beer. Catherine often came home to find him outside, with empty cans on the grass. She knew it was too much to hope that he would have the dinner ready for her when she got in. She consoled herself that Hugh was content, and he was not pestering her to only work part time. She had some independence from him at least. It suited her that he took no interest in her work, just as she'd not taken any interest in his. He'd only ever told her about his successes anyway, all the mundane details of what had happened in the office and when he'd lost potential orders, he had kept to himself. She wondered why they stayed together really, when they were living side by side more than anything else. But she loved him still and he was good man, something some of her friends weren't so lucky to have.

The calmness between them, was to be short-lived. As the days went on, Hugh became increasingly annoyed about Catherine going out to work so much, when he still had no job to go to. He hated the way she dressed so smartly, just as he put it, to sit in an office all day and soon it dawned on him that the clothes were in fact for the benefit of someone else, surely not the company. The idea grew in him until he couldn't remember when he had felt so angry. He promised himself he would find out who it was. Then they would be sorry, both of them.

He started by looking through her clothes. When he opened her wardrobe door, he was shocked by the number of different outfits she had and realised that he had never bothered to take much notice of them before. He felt in each pocket and most were empty. Two of them contained receipts from a cash machine and detailed withdrawals of thirty and forty pounds. What was most surprising was that the bank account named, was not their joint account. Why, he asked himself, did she have a separate account and what did she want the withdrawn money for? He realised she must have started making some savings of her own, probably to enable her to leave him and go off with her lover. The withdrawals could have been to pay for hotel rooms. He threw the receipts down in disgust as soon as this thought occurred to him. After a few moments he forced himself to pick them up and put them back where he had found them. He didn't want her to know he was on to her just yet, not until he had gathered more evidence.

Tomorrow was Bridget's day to come and do the housework. He had never bothered to be friendly with her, but he thought now she might know an odd fact or two that might help him piece the jigsaw together. He offered to make her a drink while she tidied the living room. She was obviously surprised by this, but never one to miss a cup of tea, she accepted.

'It's out here, when you're ready.' Hugh said and set the cups on the kitchen table. 'Why not sit down and we can have a chat eh?'

'That's kind of you Mr Walker.' Bridget sat down, unable to think what they could possibly talk about.

'You're doing a fine job here you know Bridget, and do call me Hugh.'

'It's nice of you to say so thank you.' Bridget beamed, always proud of her work.

'I don't expect you see much of my wife though do you?'

'Hardly ever. Sometimes she pops back about lunch time.'

'Really? Is she on her own then, or does she come with any of her, colleagues?' Seeing a surprised expression on Bridget's face he added, 'I'm sure she told me sometimes she brings colleagues home to get some work done in peace and quiet, away from the phone.'

'No, not while I'm here, she's always been alone. I'm only here Tuesdays and Fridays though. Anyway, she'd hardly come back for peace and quiet when I'm here to do her hoovering would she?'

'I suppose not.' he agreed. 'Does she talk about her work much, anyone she gets on well with or anything?'

'No, never says anything about it, and I don't pry. I've never been one to gossip.'

Hugh thought what a shame that was, and just nodded when she said she should be getting back to it since she'd still got the bathroom to do. He decided to see if he could find any paperwork, and more clues like the cash receipts, as soon as she had gone. If he disturbed anything accidentally and Catherine noticed, she would naturally assume that it had been done when Bridget had been dusting. He got out the drawer of the telephone table from the hall and emptied the contents into to the floor. It contained all current correspondence, the latest bills that still needed paying and bank statements. None of them gave him any clues, though he looked at the figures with interest, since it was normally Catherine who dealt with these things, he hadn't realised their gas bill was so high. He was just putting them back, when he noticed one receipt he hadn't spotted in the bottom of the drawer. It was dated the previous Wednesday and was for fifty two pounds from a restaurant in the centre of the city. Hugh had never been there.

He replaced the drawer and left the house. He got the tube to the station nearest the restaurant and walked the rest of the way. During the journey, he tried to think how he could find out conclusively who she had dined with. When he arrived, it was nearly empty and he sat down on a bar stool. He ordered a beer when the waiter asked him what he wanted.

He sat sipping it, while the waiter dried up glasses and replaced them in their rightful places.

'Are you normally this quiet?' Hugh asked.

'Only at lunch times, the evening's our busiest time.' the waiter replied.

'You might be able to help me then.'

'If I can.'

'My wife was in here recently, with a friend, and she thinks she left her umbrella behind. This is her.' He showed a photograph of Catherine that he'd taken out of his wallet. 'Do you recognise her?'

'Yes, I do. A tall chap was with her wasn't he, with a dark beard? I've got a good memory for faces.'

'That's the one.' Hugh said, feeling sick as he spoke, trying to appear normal.

'But I'm afraid we've not found any umbrellas.'

'What?' Hugh said, confused.

'Your wife didn't leave her umbrella here.'

'I see, well thank you anyway.' He managed and left without finishing his drink.

As the tube train rocked him gently back and forth on his way home, he could only think that she had always said she hated beards. Tomorrow he would follow her.

When she came home, he tried to be his usual self, though she did accuse him once during the evening of snapping at her. While they ate dinner, he looked at her, trying to see what other men saw. At ten years his junior, she was still an attractive woman. Her auburn blonde hair was set gracefully around her shoulders and her large dark blue eyes gave interest to her pretty face. Never having had children, at Hugh's insistence, she had also kept her figure trim. He could see how others might be attracted to her, how he still was himself even after all their twenty-odd years of marriage. But that didn't give her any reason to be unfaithful to him, after all he had always treated her well, given her everything she had wanted. He had, until now, not questioned what she wanted. She had always agreed to what he had said, and they had lived in quiet harmony together. Or so he had thought. Before she went to bed, Catherine said she was not going into the office until lunchtime the next day. Hugh was pleased since he would be able to make plans to follow her more easily. He told her that he would be out the next morning himself at an interview.

He left the house at 11.30 and waited around the corner of the tube station entrance, three roads down from their house. It wasn't long before he saw her and ducked behind a phone box out of sight. He ran on to the train just as the doors were about to close, stood in the next compartment from her and got off again when she did. His suspicions were being confirmed with every step she took out of the station, for this was not the one closest to the office she worked in. She was obviously going to meet her lover for lunch again.

Hugh found it hard to keep up with her stiff pace, and still remain out of sight if she happened to turn around. But he stopped dead in his tracks when he saw her walking up the steps of Stanwick Stationers. They were his previous company's biggest rival, and his wife was having an affair with someone who worked there. Her double treachery could not be forgiven.

All afternoon, Hugh paced up and down the living room, drinking whisky. Every time someone walked past the front door, he thought it might be her, perhaps coming home early. When she eventually did, at her usual time, he was beyond hearing any explanation she might have offered.

'How could you do it to me?' He shouted at her as soon as she had stepped into the room.

'Do what?' She asked, surprised.

'Have an affair.' He spat the words at her.

'An affair, what are you talking about. I'm not having an affair.'

'I knew you'd deny it.' He swayed in front of her, angry that she hadn't had the decency to admit it straight away.

'Well of course I'm denying it, it isn't true. Look darling you've had too much to drink. Your imagination is getting the better of you.'

'It most certainly is not.' He shouted, 'I know what he looks like, tall with a beard. You always told me you didn't like beards.'

'I don't like them. There's been some mistake, look let's talk about this properly, when you've had a chance to calm down.'

'Calm down, why should I calm down? You're standing there lying to me and you want me to calm down?'

'You're not listening to me.' She added soothingly, 'Look let me make you some coffee.'

'You're not getting away that easily. I'll tell you how I know there's no mistake. I followed you.' He was triumphant.

For a split second, Hugh saw fear in Catherine's eyes.

'Where did you follow me?' She asked quietly.

'Stanwick Stationers.' He delivered the two words with contempt. He went on, 'Not only are you having an affair, but you're with someone who's working for my company's biggest competitor.'

'I'll tell you this for the last time Hugh. I'm not having an affair. The reason I went into the office of Stanwick's is because that's where I work.'

'What?' He couldn't believe it. 'But you told me you worked for a company that makes electrical components.'

'Well I knew you'd be upset if you knew the truth.'

'Of course I am.'

'You may as well know the whole story, since you've decided to start playing Sherlock Holmes.' Catherine was getting tired of this confrontation. 'I'm not a secretary there. I'm one of their sales representatives.'

'What do you mean you're not a secretary? Of course you are. You couldn't be a sales rep. You haven't got what it takes.'

'Well thank you for the vote of confidence in my abilities. You never did think very highly of me, did you. For your information I did start there as a secretary, I didn't think it wise that you knew who they were, I didn't want you pressurising me for inside information. I would have stayed in that job, but others recognised my potential and encouraged me. That's something you've never done. So they trained me and now that's what I do. And what's more I'm good at it.'

'I don't believe you.' He said desperately hoping it wasn't true.

'Look at this then.' She took out a business card from her purse and thrust it in front of him. She was angry herself now, all the pent-up resentment over the years, his lack of faith in her to do anything except run the house for him, it was all rushing out.

He looked down at the card and felt crushed. He suddenly thought back to all the times he had told her the work he was doing, about the preparation he was doing for his presentations. He used to leave his briefcase unlocked, and it held copies of quotes he had prepared. She could have looked at them and then gone to those companies and undercut him. He remembered the A.M.C.T. deal. He had to know if their custom had gone to Stanwick's.

'Did you get the A.M.C.T. agreement?'

'Well the company did, but I didn't have anything to do with it.' She told him. But it was too late. He had stopped listening when she said the company had got it. At the same moment the carriage clock he'd been given as a retirement present had gleamed in the sunlight at him, and he had lifted it off the mantelpiece. He raised it up above his head and brought it down hard, onto her face. He wanted to shut her up, to stop talking before she told him of how she had listened carefully to how he planned to get their custom. How she had copied down the figures behind his back and gone in with a lower offer. All reason had left him. He struck her again and again with the clock after she had fallen to the floor. Her hands no longer tried to shield him off as he rained the blows on her. Finally he stopped and looked at her. She was almost unrecognisable and unquestionably dead.

He felt sick and rushed to the bathroom where he threw up repeatedly. When he had finally finished he staggered back to the edge of the living room, his stomach aching. He saw her body lying there, her arms above her head still looking as if they were trying to protect her. Her lovely hair was now untidy and matted with blood. He started to feel sick again, so grabbed his coat and left the house.

Not knowing where he was going, he started walking, and when tired he got on a tube. It reached the end of the line, and he didn't recognise where he was. He knew he needed a drink and found himself a pub. He sat there all evening, knocking back more whisky. He tried to think what he would do with Catherine's body, where he could bury it. He didn't want to remember how she had looked but knew he would have to see her again when he took her away. He would face that tomorrow, he said to himself, now he just wanted to blot everything out.

The barman noticed he was already a long way from sober, but since he was sitting quietly in the corner minding his own business, he was happy to take his money. When closing time came, he got him to his feet, helped him put his coat on and pushed him gently out of the door.

The fresh air woke Hugh momentarily, but he desperately needed to sleep. He stumbled along the road until he came across a park. He tottered over to the hedge which surrounded it and curled up underneath. He drifted immediately into a deep sleep. When he woke in the early hours, he was aching and dazed. He walked out to the main road and without realising, stepped in front of a grocery delivery truck, giving him serious but not fatal injuries.

A few hours later, eight miles away, Bridget was letting herself into Hugh and Catherine's house, with her key.

Brotherly Love *(Andy's Tale)*

'Is Andy in the garden?' the short, lady in white asked the man next to her. He nodded and she went out to find him.

Andy was sitting on the wooden bench in front of the yellow roses. He sat without expression, his face not betraying his thoughts, his troubles. They had started when he was a boy of eight, living happily at home in a large Victorian house with his parents.

'It'll soon be your birthday, Andy, you'd better start thinking about what you would like.' his mother said, while they walked through the park. It was difficult for him to decide, there seemed so little time to play with the toys he already had, but a train set was top of his list at the moment. He told his mother this and she frowned.

'They're awfully expensive darling, isn't there anything else you'd like?'

Andy could probably have come up with quite a selection of other suitable presents, but faced with not getting what he wanted, he dug his heels in and said flatly, 'no.'

'We'll have to see.' she said, biting her lip.

They went inside the house and Andy was given his favourite tea of fish fingers and chips.

It was early evening when the day turned sour, when he overheard his mother using the telephone in the hall.

'So when is the new edition due to arrive?' she asked.

Andy hadn't been paying attention to what she'd been saying beforehand, he was engrossed in watching television, but that phrase *new edition* sent a shock through him as if he'd touched an electric wire. He could remember the day she'd used it before. She had sat him down on the sofa and with a broad grin on her face, announced there was to be a new addition to the family. Not long after, it had arrived. A screaming, wriggling smelly thing he was supposed to call his brother Robbie. And now there was to be another one. Andy didn't know how he could stand it. He didn't want the brother he'd got, let alone another one. Brothers were there to play games with, and if they were older, they could fight the bullies off at school for you. Or if you were older, you could tease them and hide their toys. But he couldn't do anything with Robbie. He was no fun to be with, throwing his food around and dribbling all over his clothes, he was disgusting, and Andy couldn't understand why his mother spent so much time with him. To go through all that again, would be more than he could bear.

Thoughts raced through his mind as to how he could stop his mother from going ahead with such an awful plan, until in a matter of moments he'd decided. If he could get rid of the first brother, she wouldn't bother replacing him. Just like when Chester had died, Andy had pleaded for another dog, but his parents had been resolute, Chester couldn't be replaced.

He listened at the door and was satisfied his mother was still talking. He went over to Robbie who was sitting on the Turkish rug, playing quietly with his brightly painted building blocks. With quite a lot of effort, he picked him up under the arms. His mother had told him often that he must make sure Robbie didn't climb on the furniture, in case he fell and hurt himself, and if she was in the room now, would have been horrified to see Andy sit Robbie on the top of the back of the armchair. With one push, Robbie toppled backwards, his chubby legs flying upwards as he fell, striking his head on the piano before hitting the polished parquet floor.

Andy scrambled onto the chair and looked over the back at the motionless body of his fifteen months old brother. His mother suddenly opened the door and rushed into the room.

'What was that noise, what's happened?' she asked and looked down to where she'd left Robbie playing.

'It wasn't my fault,' Andy started.

'What wasn't? Where's Robbie?' she went over to Andy, but he didn't need to answer. She saw the body of her youngest child and started screaming, a loud high-pitched scream. She didn't seem to pause to draw breath, she just stood there looking at Robbie, screaming. The noise brought his father downstairs.

'It wasn't my fault.' Andy said, wanting to state his case straight away. 'I was watching T.V. and he crawled up there without me noticing.'

'Yes Andy, all right, no one blames you.' His father said, not taking in the full extent of what had happened.

He put his arms around his wife and then leaned against the armchair to steady himself, when he caught sight for the first time, of the lifeless body.

As Andy lay in bed that night, he felt so pleased that he had got away with it. No one had questioned him in any detail about the incident. He'd stuck to his story, and they had believed him. He snuggled under his blankets, smiling. He did spare a thought for his mother who was sobbing next door. He expected she would get over it by tomorrow and certainly by the weekend.

When they all returned from the funeral, all dressed in new black clothes, Andy decided he should carry on as he had been for the last couple of weeks, behave himself and sit quietly. He overheard his mother talking to his Aunt Sylvia.

'Poor Andy, he must miss Robbie desperately. He's being such a brave little soldier. They used to spend quite a lot of time together.'

Andy forced himself not to grin, thinking, if only they knew how nice it was for him now that Robbie wasn't around. When all the guests had gone, his mother asked him to go up to her bedroom with her, and he went without question in the guise of his new obedient self.

'I was saving it for your birthday, but I thought you could do with cheering up now.' She pulled out a large cardboard box, containing a train set.

'It's the latest edition.'

Andy looked up at her sharply and opened his mouth, but no words came out. The latest edition she'd said, that's what he had overheard her saying on the telephone.

The woman in white called over to the other nurse, who was standing at the other end of the garden. 'Take Andy into the day room would you please, I think he's sat outside long enough.'

She leant over to Andy, 'Been out here long enough have you Andy?' He got up from the bench. Andy didn't say a word, in the same way he hadn't spoken for the last fifty-two years.

Being Covered *(Kelly's Tale)*

Kelly was staring at the dark brown living room carpet whilst Adam scrolled on his phone.

'What you looking at?' He asked, annoyed that she was just sitting there.

'I hate this carpet. It makes the room look dark and it's hard as concrete.'

'Oh, you're on about that again.' He went back to his phone. He hoped she'd get fed up in a minute and look at what to watch on the telly. He couldn't care less about the carpet. 'We can't afford it Kelly, you know that.'

'I know, I know. We can't afford anything these days.'

He wanted to say that's because she'd insisted they had a big wedding, with six bridesmaids and to have it up at Harrington Manor. But he daren't do that otherwise she'd throw his five-day stag party in Lanzarote, straight back at him. Not that he regretted that, but it had cost a packet.

'We can get a rug if you like.' He was quite pleased with the suggestion.

'That'd cost more than having the carpet replaced, to get one big enough to cover it all up.' She picked up the remote control and pressed buttons without waiting to see what was on the TV.

'Well there's no point in going on about it then is there.' He went back to his game on his phone.

'We could claim on the insurance for a new one, then it wouldn't cost us a penny. Well, just the excess.' Kelly said after a while.

'I didn't think it covered replacing something that was just worn out.'

'It doesn't.' She replied.

'Well, what do you mean then?'

'We could say it got damaged, you know spilt something on it, and then it would be accidental damage, so they'd pay for a new one.'

'That's fraud. And I can't get involved with anything dodgy when I'm selling car finance, you know that.' he said crossly.

'I knew you'd be like this. We've paid our premiums to them for three years. We didn't switch like we could have done on those comparison sites, because you left it too late each year when it was due for renewal. Every time, for three years. We could have saved loads. I'm not leaving it to you anymore, I'll do it myself.'

She stormed out of the room, and he could hear her go into the bathroom. She'd have a really long bath, topping it up umpteen times and use up all the hot water. He'd hoped they'd watch a film together, still at least he could watch one of his Deadpool ones, she hated them.

When Adam came home from work the following Thursday, he was shocked to see a burn mark in the shape of an iron, on the living room carpet. 'What the hell happened here?'

'Promise you won't be cross,' she said. 'When I rang through to make a claim, they just asked me loads of questions. And I got into the swing of it telling them about the programme I was engrossed in whilst I did the ironing. And how I missed the stand and dropped the iron straight down on the floor.'

'I told you not to get involved in anything dodgy. And why did you have to burn it for real?'

'They said I had to send them photos. I took some real ones of the carpet and tried to Photoshop 'em on the computer, but it didn't come out right. Then I got worried they could tell the difference, so I thought I had to.'

'Stupid thing to do.'

'You're not too cross are you?' She looked at him hopefully.

'What do you think?' He stared at her before leaving and slamming the front door behind him.

By the time the pale grey carpet was fitted, on top of the most expensive underlay the shop sold, Adam had forgiven Kelly. She'd promised him she'd never do anything like that again. He hadn't admitted to her how much nicer he thought the room now looked and that when he took his trainers off, it was great to sink his feet into the soft carpet.

They agreed they'd both cut back to try and save money, so they'd only have a takeaway if they were with friends and they'd both switch to vaping. It wasn't long before they had enough to have the shower room upstairs refitted. They did have to use their friend's cousin to do it, but he'd nearly finished his apprenticeship so it should have been fine.

The leak wasn't obvious to start with, until Kelly came down one morning and found the ceiling in the kitchen had a large dark stain. When the water ran down through the light fittings, they started to argue that they should have got a proper plumber in the first place. The quotes to get everything fixed were all far more than they could afford, and the nearly-finished apprentice wasn't answering his phone, their emails or his front door.

'We'll just have to claim on the insurance. It'll be worth it, even after paying the excess.' Adam said.

'The premium went up last time.' Kelly replied, not really wanting to revisit all the upset she'd caused, now over a year ago, even though she was as delighted as Adam was with the carpet. 'I'll ring 'em tomorrow.'

Adam came home with fish and chips, as it was Friday, and they needed cheering up. He put the bag down when he saw she'd been crying.

'Promise you won't be cross.' She said.

'What now?'

'I rang to make the claim, but they said we weren't insured.'

'What! Is this because of the claim before? Do they know what you did?' He was getting worried now.

'No, it's not that. It wasn't renewed.'

'But you were going to sort it out from one of the comparison sites.'

'I know and I did. And I found some ever such a lot cheaper, it was going to save us loads of money.' She sniffed. 'Only...'

'Only what?' he asked.
'I forgot to set it up.'

It's all thanks to Campion *(Margery's Tale)*

If you're going to murder someone, I do think it's best if you're elsewhere when it happens. That's why I made sure I'd called round to my neighbours when he died. Clifford had been getting more and more cantankerous and I'd had enough. If he went now, after a decent mourning, I could enjoy a very nice retirement. If I left it much longer, he might have to go in a care home and then I'd lose his pension, I'd have to visit him and well, I'd still be married to him.

I'd got the idea several months ago, when he said how much he wanted me to plant some flowers outside the conservatory. I loathe gardening and if I'd had my way we'd have had shrubs in tubs that didn't need any work doing except maybe a satisfying shearing every few months. But no, that wasn't good enough for Clifford. He wanted flowers to look at he said and so we spent a fortune at the garden centre. And I spent ages soaking in the bath that night, trying to ease my aching back.

He chose most of the flowers, lots of different ones that would flower at different times. To be fair he had planned it out quite well. I just got more and more dismayed at how many were going in the trolley. That was until I saw the label for Red Campion. It reminded me of that detective. He was always helping a damsel in distress and little did he know he'd now be helping me. I popped the plant in amongst the ones Clifford had chosen.

The plants didn't realise how lucky they were to get so much of my attention. I always started with the Red Campion, deadheading as soon as the blooms had gone over, making sure the soil around the stems was damp but not water-logged. Those around it got whatever energy I had left.

The day I saw them arrive was the happiest that week. I even made Clifford his favourite dinner.

He was in the wheelchair most of the time now, his legs playing him up so much it was difficult for him to move on his own. Which I began to take advantage of more and more. I only had to have the radio on in whatever room I was in and sadly I couldn't hear him call out. Once he resorted to ringing me on my mobile, so I had to make sure I left it on the kitchen worktop if I was upstairs or in the bedroom if I was in the kitchen.

The afternoon I chose was as hot as the weather app predicted. I'd seen several outside and managed to collect two in a glass with a piece of paper underneath. Clifford had nodded off as he usually did that time of day. I poured a glass of water on the floor, shook the glass up and threw it by Clifford's feet. I rushed next door, desperate to be away when it happened. Thankfully Carole answered her door straight away and I asked if I could borrow some cinnamon as I wanted to make some rock cakes. So that's where I was when we heard him scream. I looked suitably worried and rushed back to my front door, but what a shame I'd forgotten to pick up my key. By the time we'd gone 'round the back, he was slumped over in his chair, clearly dead. That wretched allergy Clifford had to bees, what terrible luck that two had got into the conservatory.

I've moved away now but I've kept the little plastic label that was my inspiration, telling me how attracted to Red Campion, the bumblebees are.

Acknowledgements

I have been writing for just over thirty years, having been on several Arvon Foundation courses, belonged to two writing groups and attended theatre writing lessons over many months. I've been lucky enough to have had some stories published in anthologies and for all fourteen of my full length murder mystery plays, to have been performed on the amateur stage as fundraisers. I was introduced to fundraising back when I was a teenager, joining Rotaract, and later Rotary and from those connections, have been able to see the plays come to life. My love of stories and reading started when I was a child, growing up with my brother Keith, with our mum and dad who showed us much love and kindness.

Having decided I wanted to put my favourite stories together in a collection, I asked for help from my friend Adrian Burroughs and my daughter Emma Tuohy. They helped sift through them and gave invaluable feedback as to what would and wouldn't work. Most importantly they gave me the confidence to bring two collections together, one for crime and the other about life's dramas, for which I am very grateful.

Throughout my adult life, I've been able to do so much writing, alongside working at an advice agency, thanks to the continued support from my dear husband Nigel Tuohy, who I am indebted to.

I would like to thank my beta readers for helping me make the stories the best they can be. I really appreciate all the encouragement and time they've given me. They are fellow writers Sue Turbett, Steve Goodlad, Ruth McCracken and Penny Canvin, and my friends Adrian Burroughs and Jim Filer.

Thank you for choosing to read A Little Crime at Bedtime. I hope it didn't keep you awake.

Karen Banfield

Printed in Great Britain
by Amazon